THE TICKET

by
DEBRA COLEMAN JETER

FIREFLY
SOUTHERN FICTION
LIGHTHOUSE PUBLISHING OF THE CAROLINAS

Praise for *THE TICKET*

Complex characters . . . Jeter's coming-of-age novel considers the problems that might follow a sudden windfall.

~**Publishers Weekly**

The Ticket is a story that aches to be read. In Tray Dunaway, Debra Coleman Jeter has created a character who feels as real as you or me, with doubts, joys, problems, and dreams that seem unreachable. Watch as Tray reaches out, latches on, and starts becoming the beautiful woman she will be.

~**Ronald Kidd**
Author of *Night on Fire* and *Monkey Town*

The characters in this book are unique, interesting and possess strong potential to be memorable. A grandmother who longs to fix mistakes from her youth and find independence, a mentally unbalanced mother, and a daughter who lacks the confidence to pursue her dreams . . . quite a mix with amazing dynamics. The story abounds with tensions and conflict . . . has a strong sense of developing authorial voice.

~**Kim Peterson**
Writer-in-Residence
Bethel College

A multiform narrative tale of sudden wealth and the extraordinary woes it can bring upon an ordinary family.

~**William Kowalski**
Author of *The Adventures of Flash Jackson & The Hundred Hearts*

The Ticket takes a compelling look at a young teenage girl who believes her life is going to change for the better. The story offers up riveting drama. One would be hard-pressed not to root for the likable protagonist and hope that her story eventually ends with a happy ending. There are some authentic life lessons and talking points to be had here. All in all, this is an enjoyable debut by Jeter.

~ **RT Book Reviews**

THE TICKET BY DEBRA COLEMAN JETER
Published by Firefly Southern Fiction
an imprint of Lighthouse Publishing of the Carolinas
2333 Barton Oaks Dr., Raleigh, NC, 27614

ISBN: 978-1-941103-86-9
Copyright © 2015 by Debra Coleman Jeter
Cover design by Goran Tomic
Interior design by Karthick Srinivasan

Available in print from your local bookstore, online, or from the publisher at: www.lighthousepublishingofthecarolinas.com

For more information on this book and the author visit: www.karencampbellprough.com

All rights reserved. Non-commercial interests may reproduce portions of this book without the express written permission of Lighthouse Publishing of the Carolinas, provided the text does not exceed 500 words. When reproducing text from this book, include the following credit line: "*The Ticket* by Debra Coleman Jeter, published by Lighthouse Publishing of the Carolinas. Used by permission."

Commercial interests: No part of this publication may be reproduced in any form, stored in a retrieval system, or transmitted in any form by any means—electronic, photocopy, recording, or otherwise—without prior written permission of the publisher, except as provided by the United States of America copyright law.

This is a work of fiction. Names, characters, and incidents are all products of the author's imagination or are used for fictional purposes. Any mentioned brand names, places, and trademarks remain the property of their respective owners, bear no association with the author or the publisher, and are used for fictional purposes only.

Brought to you by the creative team at Lighthouse Publishing of the Carolinas: Eva Marie Everson, Jessica R. Everson, and Deb Haggerty.

Library of Congress Cataloging-in-Publication Data
Debra Coleman Jeter.
The Ticket /Debra Coleman Jeter 1st ed.

Printed in the United States of America

For there is hope for a tree, if it is cut down, that it will sprout again, and that its tender shoots will not cease.

Job 14:7 (NKJV)

PROLOGUE

The mind is its own place, and in itself
Can make a heav'n of hell, a hell of heav'n
John Milton
Paradise Lost

My name is Tray, and I live in Paradise, Kentucky.

They say Kentucky is known for its fast horses and beautiful women. The joke is maybe it should be beautiful horses and fast women. Neither applies to the women in my family, except maybe Mama. She's definitely beautiful, but she isn't fast. At least not normally, though she can be when she's in one of her manic states. But those aren't beautiful. In fact, they are downright ugly.

"How'd this town ever come to have a name like Paradise?" I used to ask Gram when I was little. Enough times I got to know her version of the story pretty much by heart. It goes like this:

"It started at a crossroads where there was a little store owned by a man name of Sullivan, and folks just called it Sullivan's Stop. Some folks got there by foot, others by stage coach, and a lot by horse and buggy. It was on the turnpike between Paducah, Kentucky, and Nashville, Tennessee.

"One day, a rascal of a fellow came to Sullivan's Stop and began challenging the men unlucky enough to be there that day with a pair of dice. Pretty soon he owned Sullivan's store, and he discovered the men around there were such easy marks for his pair of dice, he started expanding. Before long, there was a blacksmith shop and a tavern, even a hotel. A bustling community, folks called it Pair o' Dice.

"Then one day a traveling preacher came to town. He preached hellfire and brimstone, and showed the local folks the error of their ways: the sin of gambling. So when the church was built, they changed the spelling to Paradise."

Even though I knew the answer to my next question, I'd ask it anyway. "Did you know those men yourself, Gram?"

She would laugh her deep-throated chuckle and her blue eyes would crinkle with amusement. "I may be old, child, but I haven't lived forever."

She changed up the words in the story a little from one telling to the next, but you get the gist. Now I don't know if there's any truth in the tale or not. But for a time the year I was fourteen, I thought the name might suit us after all. I'd never had much in the way of luck, and I was tired of being too tall, too bony, too uncoordinated. Then something unimaginable happened, and it looked like all our lives were set to change for the better.

CHAPTER ONE

"... The lottery was a great charity, the friend of the people, a vast beneficent machine that recognized neither rank nor wealth nor station ... Invariably it was the needy who won, the destitute and starving woke to wealth and plenty, the virtuous toiler suddenly found his reward in a ticket bought at a hazard."

> **Frank Norris**
> McTeague: A Story of San Francisco
> 1899

Paradise, Kentucky
September 1975

I AM CONTENT, curled on the sofa with the afternoon light streaming in through the picture windows, warming me as I allow myself to be carried away to Egypt, where I am a beautiful, dark-skinned, blue-eyed spy deeply in love with a dashing adventurer. But, even more, I am deeply committed to my cause and uncertain on which side of the political fracas my love's true allegiance lies. I must not—I cannot—be swept totally by the passion that threatens to consume my soul . . .

So when my father charges through the door, reeking of stale coffee and fatigue, I momentarily forget who or where I am and am taken by surprise.

THE TICKET

I look up, and our eyes meet. He sighs and turns away without a word. Then he whirls back to face me. He strides to my side, jerks the book from my hands, throws it on the floor so that I cry out.

"Why aren't you outside playing like any normal kid?" he barks. "What's the matter with you?"

Before I can think of a reply—I am still in transit, being jerked from the beauty and passion of the Nile spy to the awkwardness of my fourteen-year-old body—he is gone, leaving me bookless and defenseless. In that instant, the real me is back: pale skin splattered with angry, reddish acne spots, frizzy dark hair, long, narrow face, thin legs and arms.

I blink back tears and bend to retrieve the discarded book, smooth out the new crease in its spine. Then I fling it back to the floor, trying not to cringe when it slaps the worn beige carpet at a precarious angle.

"Gram," I moan. My long skinny legs assume a life of their own, carrying me to the refuge of my grandmother's room, where I flop onto Gram's bed with a heavy sigh.

"What's wrong, Tray?" Gram quickly hides her snuff brush and can, but not before I catch a glimpse and a whiff of tangy, gooey tobacco juice.

"Nothing." I rise up on my elbows to look at her. She's responsible for a lot of my features. The same long, narrow face, lined now with years of hard work and worry; the same thin legs and arms, beginning to sag the way mine probably will some day; the same dark hair, still thick, but threaded with silver.

Silence. Gram sews a while. Her fingers whip the needle in and out, in and out, of the tiny garment she is stitching. Gram's sewing is not the greatest. She sews some of my school clothes. The other kids can tell they're homemade, and they make fun of me. I hate those kids for the way they make me feel. And, even more, for the way I make Gram feel when I spew, "I don't want your old tacky clothes anymore."

I love it, though, when Gram makes doll clothes because, with a little imagination, they are spectacular. The dolls provide a perfect working model for my plan to be a fashion designer. I'll create glorious ball gowns, like in a fairytale, and wedding dresses, and exotic dance costumes . . .

I tell my ideas to Gram. Sometimes I draw them too, though I'm not as good at drawing as I wish. Trying the clothes on the dolls to see how they fit is a lot like trying on different personalities for Gram. Some days I pretend to be a brainiac, testing my latest ten-dollar words from Dickens or Jane Austen. I would be afraid to do this with anyone else. But, with Gram, I can savor their flavor on my tongue.

Sometimes I pretend I'm the kind of girl who attracts all the boys. Like Scarlett O'Hara. I make up stories to tell Gram, about my beaus and what happened during recess. With Gram, I can be pretty and popular, which is the furthest thing from the truth. I know Gram sees right through my stories, but she never says so. Not like Mama, who calls me out if I stretch the truth one whit, who sees me as flawed in every way and reminds me of it every chance she gets.

"Are you sure you don't want to talk about it?"

I consider telling Gram about Dad throwing my book on the floor, but there's something else, something that bothered me even before I started reading.

"I wouldn't want to go to their stupid party anyway," I say.

"Whose party?"

I feel my lip curl. "Rita Davis, of all people."

"What do you mean by that?"

"By what?"

"Of all people."

"It's just that she's—I don't know—I mean, I do know, but it's stupid. She's even taller and skinnier than I am. I bet her arms aren't this big around." I make a circle with my thumb and index finger. "One day last week she was talking about having this party, and how she was afraid nobody would come. She was talking to me. To *me*. I mean, why was she talking to me about it if she wasn't even going to invite me?"

"I don't know. Maybe she decided not to have it or—"

THE TICKET

"No, that's not it. That's what I thought at first, when I didn't get an invitation. But then today I heard all these people talking about the party, and when I looked at Rita, she wouldn't meet my eyes. And after I was so nice to her! I'm such a spaz. S—P—A—Z." I strike my head with the palm of my hand. "I told her not to worry, that *I* would come to her party. Like she gave a flip if I would come or not. No, it's the popular kids she's after."

"Maybe it got lost in the mail or something. Why don't you ask her?"

"Are you kidding? That would be way too humiliating. Besides I know it didn't. That crowd never invites me to their dumb old parties. I just thought—but I don't know why I thought . . ."

"Thought what?"

"Thought maybe this year was going to be different."

Gram looks over the top of her spectacles, which have slid down her rather large nose so they rest just above the small brown mole on the right-hand side, not far above the nostril. "Why don't you have one of your own?"

I stare at Gram, feeling almost hopeful for a second. "Maybe I could have a party at the roller rink."

Then reality hits me, and I can tell by Gram's expression that she, too, is thinking of the cost. "It would probably be cheaper to have one here," she says.

I glance around the familiar room, seeing it with new eyes. The worn rug, the circles on the ceiling from a variety of old leaks, the chipped paint on the little bedside table, the faded Bible, Gram's snuff can and spit cup. Of course, we wouldn't necessarily be in *this* room, but still . . .

I think of my mother. "It wouldn't work," I say, rolling over onto my back and staring at the swirly brown patterns in the ceiling, like spilled coffee on a dingy sheet. "Even if it weren't for Mama, I don't know if anybody would come. And if they did, and if she had one of her moods or something, I could never look at anyone again."

"I suppose it's too risky," Gram says, and I can tell from the disappointment in her voice that she knows I'm right.

"They're all so stupid anyway, with their expensive clothes and shoes, and their pretentious banter: *Where did you get those buffalo sandals and toe socks—they're out of sight!*" I mimic one of the girls in my class, Debbie Worthington, making her sound even more nasal and ridiculous than she really is.

"What are buffalo sandals and toe socks?" Gram goes back to her stitching.

I start to explain that they're these goofy leather sandals with wedge heels and four straps, but I figure Gram doesn't really need to know the details. I break off and stare at her blankly, picturing the stupid toe socks in my mind, which are just what they sound like. Every toe has its own shape, like gloves for your feet. I wouldn't wear them even if somebody *gave* me a pair.

"I tell you, Gram, it's the dumbest fashion I ever saw in my entire life." I sigh and roll over on my side to look at her. "Anyway, I wouldn't have any fun if I did go to their old party. That's why I said it was nothing. Because it *is* nothing. It just makes me feel like such a spaz remembering how nice I was to Rita."

"It's nothing to be ashamed of. Being nice is not a sin, you know."

"Yes, it is!"

"Come here, sweetheart." Gram sets her sewing aside, pats her lap. I go to her and put my head in her lap, inhaling the familiar smells of Jergens lotion and snuff. She runs cool fingers through my hair, fingers that are beginning to gnarl like the old dogwood tree in our backyard.

"You're going to be a knockout someday, you know. You just have to be a little bit patient. Your day is coming. I'm sure of that."

"Oh, Gram, you always say that."

"Only because it's true. Now run along and do your chores."

Someday. *Someday.* Doesn't Gram know anything? Someday doesn't matter. Someday isn't here, may never be here. All that matters, all that I can feel, is now. And now is pathetic. Now *stinks.* What can I do about now?

Well, for one, I have chores to do. I leave Gram and saunter into the kitchen where I put away the last of the dishes from the drainer, slamming the cabinet door shut so hard the plates inside rattle. If only I had some decent clothes, something stylish, something that would deserve a grudging compliment, if not outright envy. We aren't all that poor. I know we aren't. My dad's just stingy, and I hate him for it.

I return to my bedroom and switch on my turntable. I stand and gaze glumly into my closet. The rows of bargain basement clothes—their sleeves or legs too short—stare back. I reach for the well-worn catalog from Tall Sophisticates, which I hide under my bed like a boy hiding his dirty magazines, not wanting Dad to catch me lusting after *that ridiculously overpriced merchandise.*

Not long ago, I made the mistake of showing a favorite outfit to my mother. "Isn't it cute?" I'd said, hoping for . . . *what?*

"Mm. A bit old for you, don't you think? I mean, those models are fully developed. It wouldn't look like that on you."

I turn to the picture I'd once loved—a coppery shift that clings to the model's chest and slim hips, catches the light and shimmers with a promise of gold, a hint of lavender.

That ensemble is tarnished now by the memory of Mama's nonchalant dismissal, so I flip to another favorite. The model, tall and thin with dark hair like mine, leans casually against a fat white column. Her lips are parted in a dreamy smile and the soft blue cashmere sweater clings to the curves of her chest. Her breasts are small, yet alluring. *Powder blue*, the catalog says. I like the sound of that, though I wonder what it means. Who would put on blue powder?

I imagine myself as a famous designer, the head of a creative team. "I'm not sure about the neckline," I say to those standing around, just waiting for my opinion. "Perhaps it would work better with something less round, something more angular, off the shoulders even, like this." I quickly sketch the neckline as I envision it, and my assistants nod their approval.

I stand, catalog in hand, and walk to the mirror on my bedroom dresser. There's an ugly pimple just below my lip. I dab a bit of medicated acne cream on the spot, crinkling my nose at the smell. Still clutching the catalog, I lift my shirt and stare at my bony chest. I suck in my stomach and expand my chest. I frown at my reflection; the effort only makes my ribs stick out more than they already do.

I look away, close my eyes and, inside my mind, my breasts swell to the size and shape of the catalog model's. Okay, a little larger. For good measure.

The phone rings because, in my imagined world, the phone rings all the time. I snatch the receiver and say a casual hello.

"Tonight?" My tone says: *short notice*. "Oh, I don't think I can make it. I'm pretty busy."

A sudden rapping on my door causes me to start. My eyes pop open, my breasts deflate, and the imaginary conversation shrivels on my breath.

"Tray? Who are you talking to in there?"

Dad.

I tuck in my shirt hurriedly. The door swings open before I can answer, and he enters. His face wears the expression that means he's trying to figure out how to say something, and I cringe at what's coming.

"Nobody," I mumble. "Must be the record player." I look over at the turntable where Rod Stewart blares out a lyric about handbags and glad rags. I rush to turn the volume down.

"What's that?" Dad points to the catalog.

Still clutching it to my chest, I look down guiltily. "This? Oh, this is—nothing, really. Just a catalog."

Dad seems to accept this explanation, and I'm not sure whether to be relieved or disappointed.

"Tray, the thing is . . . I don't know how to say this, but . . . I'm sorry about—you know, earlier today. I guess I was just frustrated about something else, and I took it out on you." He sits on the edge of my bed and fingers the quilt Gram made for my last birthday. It's a wedding ring pattern and I have not told Gram that the thought of wedding rings depresses me because I know no one in his right mind will ever want to marry this bony-breasted girl.

I shrug. "It's all right."

"No, it isn't. I shouldn't be so—I just want what's best for you, and I worry that you read too much when you should be out having fun."

"It's all right," I say again because how can I explain that I would like to be out having fun too but I have no one to have fun *with*?

"I worry that books are a way of escaping reality," he continues.

Well, yeah . . . exactly. I look at my father's handsome face, a faint vertical line marring his forehead now. He has no idea what it's like to be unpopular. He and Mama, with their compact, attractive figures and natural good looks, have produced a changeling in me. I see no possible way to bridge the gap.

He rises from the bed and moves toward the door, straightening his shoulders just a bit as if in rebuttal of the defeat in his voice.

"I know, Dad," I say, almost feeling sorry for him. Then I make an abrupt decision. I open the catalog at random. "Dad, do you suppose I might be able to order some new clothes?"

He turns back and glances at the catalog I'm holding out to him. He takes it and moves an index finger across the page to find the price. His eyes widen slightly, and I know he's found it. He looks again, as if double checking the number of digits. He stands stock still. His silence strikes me as more expressive than words, as though he is listening with every fiber of his being. Like a cat whose fur lifts in the presence of an animal intruding upon his territory.

A page flutters to the floor, and I reach down to pick it up.

"What do you have there?" He glances at my drawing of a sweater with a different neckline.

I turn the page facedown on the dresser. "It's nothing. Just some scribbles. The thing is—I do sort of need some new clothes. I know these are pretty expensive," I rush to say, "but I thought—"

He slams the catalog shut with a grunt. "Tray, I wish we could afford to buy clothes like that. But we can't. It's hard for me to believe anyone can pay those kinds of prices." He shakes his head, his face a mix of wonder and frustration, and I wish I had not asked.

"It's okay, Dad."

"I hate to tell you how many days sometimes go by before I get an insurance commission large enough to buy even one of those outfits." He thumps the catalog, hard. "By the time I do, we're behind on so many bills; it's already spent."

"I know you work hard," I say.

"You're darned right; I work hard. But that doesn't seem to matter very much, does it?" He sighs. "I'm sorry for laying all this on you—you shouldn't have to think about any of this, but it burns me—it really does—how many people there are who work no harder than I do and who can order clothes like that without thinking twice."

He thumps the catalog once more and turns to go, his back conveying both indignation and disappointment. My eyes go to a spot on the back of his head where the hair is beginning to thin.

Alone again, I turn the volume up on Rod Stewart. I pick up the needle and set it back to the beginning of the song. In "Handbags and Gladrags," the girl's grandfather had to sweat to buy her stuff. My Grampa would have loved buying nice things for me, I just know it—if only he'd lived long enough. But he was taken too soon, from me and from Gram, before I was old enough to care a gritty Fig Newton about clothes.

THE TICKET

CHAPTER TWO

IN THE SCHOOL cafeteria, my toes bump the ends of my K-Mart buddies. I stare at the back of Debbie Worthington, who has just breezed past me as if I'm invisible. Whereas my legs are long sticks, Debbie's calves curve seductively in her new red knee socks. I wonder how she keeps her socks from wrinkling or sagging around her ankles the way mine always do.

A quick glance to the floor and, yep, Debbie's sneakers are bright white Nikes.

Outside, the day is hot and sultry as the middle of summer when you're mostly wearing shorts, tube tops, and flip-flops. I imagine sweat circles darkening the armpits of Debbie's red turtle-necked sweater. The navy pleated skirt completes her tricolor. Next year is the big bicentennial celebration: 1776 to 1976. Already the stores are gearing up with loads of everything in red, white, and blue. Not that I've been able to buy any of it.

I wonder if I can piece together something from my own closet in red, white, and blue. I do own a red pleated skirt, but I've had it for several years. It was way too short last year, and I just keep growing.

Maybe Gram could sew something good for me after all.

I reach down to scratch the mosquito bite on my ankle before pulling up my off-white knee socks, knowing they will sag again the minute I take a single step. When I look up, I nearly catch the eye of Rita Davis. I glance away and hope Rita's party was a dismal failure. My skin flushes with guilt the way it always does when I have a mean thought.

Rita is joining Debbie and the other popular girls at "their" table. They're laughing, resplendent in their new fall wardrobes. Funny, how similar they are, I tell myself. It's as if they all shopped at the same store on the same day. I hesitate, trying to summon my courage to join them.

What's the big risk—their laughter dies? No, worse, they turn on me.

I can't do it.

I sink into a chair at an empty table. The food on my tray stares unappetizingly back at me. Rubbery gelatin with squares of some kind of pinkish fruit in it, pasty mashed potatoes, a thin slab of greasy meat in thick white gravy, and a slice of white bread.

Yum.

I should have asked Gram to send me something I could eat, one of her homemade pimento cheese sandwiches or bologna on saltines. I try rubbing some of the disgusting gravy off the meat. I've never understood what they mean by chicken-fried steak; is it chicken or is it steak? I know one thing about it: it's supposed to be tender, but it's not. I saw on it for a while, but it's so tough, I give up. I pull the milk carton open, take a sip and make a face. Lukewarm, and I can barely stand milk when it's icy cold. I push my tray aside and open my novel, trying to look too involved to be lonely. It's my usual lunchtime ritual.

"Excuse me."

I look up to see the new girl from English class standing uncertainly with the toe of one penny loafer pressed on top of the other. "Do you mind if I sit here?"

I gulp, swallowing the mouthful of warm milk, and trying not to grimace. "Sure." The girl still hesitates, so I add, "So what are you waiting for?"

The girl's mouth breaks into a wide smile, revealing wide metal braces. "I wasn't sure if you meant, sure, sit down, or sure, you minded."

"Oh." I grin back. "Sometimes I like to be a bit abstruse."

"Or maybe I'm just a little obtuse," the girl counters.

My mouth nearly drops open.

She seats herself beside me and starts setting out the items from a red, white, and blue lunch box decorated in stars and stripes. A sandwich, a bag of carrots and celery pieces, and another bag with something green in it that looks like a large pickle.

"I can't believe you knew what I meant. I'm not even sure abstruse is the right word."

"I'm not all that sure about obtuse either," says the girl.

We both laugh. "So, you like to read?" I ask.

The girl nods. "All the time."

"I'm Tray Dunaway."

"I'm Lori Penman. I'm new here."

I know that. I've seen her in class and in the hallways. If I'm honest though, what with her smart wardrobe and petite figure, I assumed she'd be automatically welcomed into the popular crowd. "Where did y'all move here from?"

As soon as the words are out of my mouth, I want to bite them back. Saying "y'all" makes me sound like a Southern hick. Lori doesn't seem to notice. "Alabama," she says.

Alabama, really? That's farther south than Kentucky. "You don't sound Southern," I point out.

"That's probably because we weren't there all that long. We've lived all over the place."

"So . . . is it hard being new?" I feel myself flush again, realizing it's just as hard, maybe harder, being unpopular and *not* new, not even having the excuse of newness.

Lori shrugs. "I guess. Sometimes I think it's just hard being me."

I absorb this while silence falls between us. We're checking each other out but trying not to be too obvious about it. Lori wears glasses *and* braces, but she's really pretty anyway. She has dark blonde, almost honey-colored hair. It's cut in a stylish way with side-swept bangs, and a sort of winged effect on the sides that probably cost a mint, and her nose is very small and turns up just a tiny bit on the end. Her pink-framed glasses are so big, and her face is so small, I feel like I'm looking at her through a store window. What I can see of her skin, though, tells me she never had a day of acne in her life. Her face is round, like her glasses, with a hint of a dimple in one cheek, just waiting for her to smile.

To break the silence, because seriously, I cannot waste this opportunity, I ask, "What else do you like to do—besides read?"

Lori shrugs. "I don't know." She hesitates but then brightens as she adds, "I like to travel."

"Really?" I've never been friends with anyone who went anywhere more exotic than Florida for summer vacation. "Have you traveled a lot?"

Lori blushes. "We *move* a lot, but that doesn't really count. I haven't traveled anywhere exciting. Not yet. Except through books. But I'd like to someday."

I sigh. "That's the nice thing about books, isn't it? For a time, you can be someone altogether different. Like an athlete or a film star, or even someone who's on the short side. Petite, like you."

"I don't know why you'd want to be short. Someday you'll be glad that you're tall, I bet." Lori draws her sandwich from its bag, then slaps it back on top. "What kind of athlete would you be?"

"Oh, I could never be an athlete for real. I'm way too uncoordinated. But I can pretend. I read this book called *Champion's Choice*. It's about a champion tennis player, and the author is always describing her tennis ensembles—even her socks and the ribbon in her hair and the way it all coordinates. That's another thing I like a lot. Fashion. I'm going to be a fashion designer someday." I look down at my outdated skirt and blouse. "Not that you can tell it by looking at me."

"I think you look fine," Lori says.

"No, I don't. Your clothes are so much more stylish."

"My mom likes to shop," she says, and an odd look passes through her round eyes as if she's about to add something. Everything about her is round—her face, eyes, glasses, arms. Maybe it's because my own face and body are so long and thin that I totally love the roundness of Lori's features.

I wait, but she is silent. "That's awesome," I say, because somebody needs to say something. "I can only dream of a mother like that."

Lori still says nothing, but the oddly unsettled expression in her eyes persists. So, I plunge on. "My dad hates it that I read so much. He thinks there's something wrong with me."

"That must be awful for you," Lori says, her eyes sympathetic. "Escaping into another world is one of my favorite things in life."

I peer at Lori. I've been figuring she might be my friend for a day or two, at best, but sure the popular girls would claim her within a week. Now, though, a surge of hope sweeps through me. Maybe Lori *is* different from them, different enough that she'll fit better with me than with any of the others. I glance over at the table where the popular girls sit and realize, with a start, that they're staring right back with a mixture of scorn and curiosity at me and Lori.

"Are you thinking I'm really weird?"

I shake my head without hesitation. "No weirder than I am, just more honest."

Lori nibbles at the sandwich, which is on whole wheat bread with the crusts cut off. It looks good, and my stomach growls.

"Want half?"

I shake my head, even as my mouth starts to water.

"Come on. I never eat both halves."

What the hay. I reach for the half sandwich being offered and sink my teeth into the soft bread. "Mmm. Cheese and tomato?" I say between quick bites.

"And butter." Lori takes a bite of celery. The sound of her munching blares out in the lunchroom, which has become inconveniently quiet. Heads twist in our direction. Lori blushes again, and, I can't help it, a wave of laughter engulfs me.

"I'm sorry," I manage to get out. "It's just—that's the sort of thing that always happens to me."

Lori holds out a hand in protest. She covers her mouth as she bursts into laughter right along with me. "I don't want to spew

THE TICKET

celery all over you," she says from behind her hand.

"It's really not that funny," I say, which only makes us laugh harder. It feels so good having someone to laugh with. We laugh until tears come. Lori has to remove her glasses to dab at her eyes.

That's when I get to see what she looks like for real. Her eyes are a beautiful hazel color, with a heavy fringe of long black lashes. "How come your eyelashes are so black?" I ask before I have a chance to think about it. "Do you use mascara?"

"Me?" Lori squeaks. She sounds like a chipmunk. We are off again, and now it's our laughter drawing glances from other tables.

When we finally get our bearings, I say, "I mean, look at my hair, it's way darker than yours, and my eyelashes are nothing like that dark."

Lori grimaces. "I'd rather have black hair than black eyelashes."

"Really?" I mean, really?

"Sure. How many people actually look at your eyelashes anyway? Especially if you wear glasses." She puts the enormous pink glasses back on. "And if you want black eyelashes, mascara is probably not as hard as it looks."

"Have you ever tried it?"

"Nope."

"Of course not." Stupid question; she doesn't need it. But I have the delicious feeling that Lori is the kind of person I can say stupid things to without kicking myself afterward. "Well, I've tried it and I stuck the darned thing right in my eyeball. No beauty pageants for me."

Lori giggles. For just a second, I wonder if my new friend laughs too much or too easily and if I'm going to get tired of laughing after a while. I don't think so.

"Say," says Lori, "do you want to go shopping with me and my mom on Saturday? We're looking for new fall clothes."

I am at once thrilled and filled with misgivings. Happy to be asked. Fearful I won't be allowed to go or, if I am, not given any money to spend. "I'll see if I can," I mumble.

After lunch, Lori waves as we head in separate directions for afternoon classes. Debbie Worthington brushes past me, her knee socks still smooth and taut over her curvy legs. This time I hardly feel any envy, in spite of the fact that my left sock is bunching around my ankle. I have plans of my own now. And things will work out, as Gram always says. Somehow they will.

THE TICKET

CHAPTER THREE

The shopping day dawns bright and sunny, but there's a cool breeze singing through the hickory trees to keep it bearable. I skip with pure joy as Lori, her mom, and I march through the store, pausing to look at anything and everything, irrespective of price tags. Lori's mom has a trim, petite figure, and at first, I admit, I feel gawky and unattractive in her presence. But unlike mine, Lori's mother sees my height, long neck, and arms, and legs, as something to envy, something to show off rather than hide. She practically has me believing in my own potential.

But then I'm standing in front of the all-too-revealing mirrors in the department store, staring at my tall, bony image. My confidence slips right off me, crawls up under one of the circular clothing racks, looks for an escape route, and out it goes.

"I look like a giraffe," I say, disgusted at the sight of my knees in a mini-length, geometrically patterned, black-and-white skirt-and-sweater set.

"You do no such thing," says Lori's mom. Her name is Julia and she's asked me to call her that, too. Which is hard for me to remember, but I try. "Here, try this one."

She's pulled a beautiful pleated skirt from the rack and holds the hanger at my waist. The skirt is an unusual shade of blue, almost lavender.

My mouth waters at the sight of it, but I've already checked

THE TICKET

the price of the skirts on that rack. I can't afford even the skirt, much less a complete outfit. I shake my head.

"What's wrong? You don't like it?"

"It's not that . . . it's just . . ." I grimace at what I'm about to say. "It's so expensive."

Julia seems totally nonplussed by such a statement. "Well, it doesn't cost anything to try it on, does it? With your cloud of dark hair, I just know you'll be surprised at the effect. You're better off, you know, to have a few nice things than a closet full of marginal stuff."

I nod, absorbing the lesson in case it might ever be relevant, not wanting to admit that I can't afford even *one* "nice" thing, much less a *few*. Reluctant but excited too, I try on the skirt with a matching sweater, come out of the dressing room, and pirouette for Lori and her mom.

Julia looks at me critically for a moment or two, and then her face breaks into a small, approving smile, a dimple appearing in her right cheek. "Perfect," she says. "The shade is perfect with your eyes and skin tone. I have an eye for these things, trust me."

I bask in the compliment. Everything in me longs for the outfit, to make it my own. I stare at myself in the mirror as if for the first time. Instead of the flaws I usually focus on—the frizzy hair, the bird-like neck, the blemishes in my complexion—I see the glow that self-confidence can create. My dark hair is a kind of halo around my flushed face, my eyes sparkle, my full lips curve slightly. And then reality, in the shape of the meager dollars in my pocketbook, zooms in and, once again, I shake my head.

"I think I'll look around a little more."

Julia shrugs, accepting my words—I guess maybe she suspects the reason?—and begins thumbing through the racks, pulling out a skirt here and there, searching for the right top to match. Some in her own size, some in Lori's, and a few in mine.

I finally locate a pretty skirt and sweater in my size on a sale rack, stuck in amongst lots of ugly stuff, that actually falls within my meager budget. The sweater is a fuzzy yellow, the skirt a yellow and baby blue plaid on a cream background. Powder blue? Could *this* be powder blue? I try them on and model for Lori and Julia, almost fearful of their reaction. I so want this to be the right choice.

Julia looks doubtful. "I think you look better in pleats than in that A-line," she says. "And I'm not sure yellow is your color."

So, I return the skirt and sweater to its rack. Later, however, before we leave the store, having found nothing else within my budget I like enough to try on, I retrieve the yellow and blue outfit and, almost furtively, carry it to the check-out register. I catch Julia's eye on me and start to speak, to defend my choice. But, not knowing how to explain that sometimes you have to "settle," I say nothing at all.

Julia smiles. "A girl who knows her own mind," she says. "An altogether admirable quality."

And just like that, I feel better. But not for long because, deep down, I know the compliment is false. The salesgirl rings up the purchase, and I pay in cash, wondering if Julia can see I've exhausted the funds in my pocketbook.

Behind her at the check-out counter, Julia places a large stack of selections on the counter. I gasp. "You're buying all of those?"

Simultaneously, the salesgirl, who has thin lips and a slightly protruding chin, says, "Will that be all?"

Julia glances back toward the racks, then at me. "Why don't you let me buy you that other outfit, the one that looked so good on you?"

I hesitate, yearning for the clothes, but unable to accept charity. "Thank you, but no," I say. "I couldn't possibly."

"Are you sure? It looked so heavenly on you; it would be my pleasure."

"I'm sure," I say, wanting to cry. The salesgirl looks impatient, and the moment of opportunity passes.

"That's all, then," says Julia, and the girl rings up the purchases.

I am staggered at the total, but Julia doesn't flinch, merely takes out her checkbook and scribbles the information into the blanks.

"Look at this!" Lori beckons to me. I leave the register,

carrying the bag with my skirt and sweater in it, which feels like I'm hauling lead. Next thing I know, I'm oohing and aahing over a rack of party dresses: long gowns with sequins, some strapless, a glimmering blue-silver one with a strap over one shoulder, dresses for a ball or a prom. And I wonder if ever in my lifetime I will wear such a dress, much less design one. I finger the glimmering garment, search for the price tag, which is tucked away discreetly. I look again, count the number of digits before and after the decimal.

No way will I ever own a dress like that.

Lori glances toward the check-out register, where her mother appears to be involved in a quiet conversation with the salesgirl. "Oh, dear," she says, "not that again."

"What?"

"We haven't lived here that long, so I was hoping it would be okay."

"What do you mean?"

Lori lowers her voice, so I have to bend to hear. "Sometimes they have a list of people not to accept checks from, and sometimes she's on that list." Lori sighs. "But I didn't even know she'd been here before."

I glance from Lori to her mother. Julia's face is pale, but her shoulders are high as she heads toward us.

"My mother's great, but she's also sort of delusional," Lori mutters.

"Mine too," I say, flushing guiltily. Is *delusional* the right word for Mama? I don't think so, but what is?

"Always remember your posture, girls," Julia says, "whatever befalls you." She makes no further reference to the fact that she has left all her purchases on the counter, and Lori doesn't ask. A wave of embarrassment for my new friend and her mother washes over me.

A few minutes later, we are trying different fragrances at the cosmetic counter, and to my amazement, both Lori and her mom seem to have forgotten the incident. They are laughing and chatting, and I find myself suddenly, surprisingly witty. We leave the store with only my meager purchase, but in a spirit of comradeship that is, for me, new and delightful.

Julia is not in a hurry to take me home, and I'm happy to make the day last longer. So I let them persuade me to go to their house for a while.

It's getting dark by the time Julia takes me home. After she pulls her car into my driveway, she and Lori wait in the car until I have opened the front door.

"I hope your mom likes your new clothes," Lori calls from the car.

"So do I," I say, though I'm not sure she can hear me. I wave goodbye and square my shoulders.

I find my mother in her bedroom with the door closed and the lights off, which I flip on. She lets out a little groan.

"Mama? Are you okay?"

Her back is to me, and she doesn't bother to turn over. She's wearing a faded red silk nightgown, and her dark-blonde hair is in a major tangle. On the bedside nightstand are an array of pill bottles and a glass half full of water.

The drapes, which consist of one gray panel and one black, are completely drawn shut. I resist the urge to pull them open. A crumpled tissue next to the pills suggests she's either been crying or blowing her nose or both.

"No, I'm not okay," she says, as though whatever is wrong is my fault.

"What's wrong?"

"It's my head."

Again? I give a little sigh, wondering if maybe, just maybe, my recent purchase could brighten things. We'll have a mother-daughter moment, in spite of the signs suggesting otherwise. "Do you want to see my new outfit?"

She is silent for so long I eventually turn to leave. Her voice reaches me just as I get to the door. "Go ahead. Show me if you must. And then—*please*—turn off the light."

Don't do me any favors, I think, tempted to keep on walking. Later, I'll wish I had. But some self-destructive urge keeps

THE TICKET

prompting me to seek the woman's approval.

So I reach into the bag and pull out my new clothes. "I can try them on for you if you'd like," I offer, that stubborn kernel of hope still alive.

Mama has risen on one elbow and turned her body toward me now. She glances at the skirt and sweater dangling at my side. Then she sinks back into the bed, clutching her head as though the effort—or the sight of my purchase—has increased the pain almost beyond endurance.

"Don't bother. I can see the color's wrong for you."

"Fine," I snap. "If you only knew what I went through to find something that wasn't too—oh, *never mind*." I slam the door, thinking I don't *care* if the sound makes her headache worse.

But in my next breath, I remember the lights, even before hearing, "I told you to turn off the lights." Her intonation is somehow both flat and sharp at the same time.

For a second, I consider ignoring the voice, pretending not to hear. But then the familiar tingling flush of guilt tells me I should feel more sympathy for my mother's condition. Haven't I been reminded often enough? I open the door, flip the light switch off.

"Don't mind me, Tray." My mother's voice is faint. "I'm just so . . . so depressed and so tired of this headache. I'm sure the clothes will be fine."

I close the door, more gently this time. A perverse impulse makes me want to try the outfit on for my mother even now, but I know better than to disturb her again. A brighter thought comes. Gram. I will try it on for Gram. Not that there will be any real information there—Gram would claim to like it even if she didn't.

And perhaps, after all, that is exactly what I want.

I drag the clothes on as if Mama's depression has invaded my body. I look in the mirror and hate my choices, hate my body, and hate the predictability of Gram's reaction. I slump into the den where Gram is watching some mindless television show. She looks in my direction and rises with a faint groan to switch off the set. There's a brownish smudge near the corner of her mouth, almost certainly a snuff stain.

"So what do you think?" I ask, deliberately sounding like I don't much care.

"The clothes are lovely," Gram says, "but what's with the long face?"

I sink onto Gram's bed, wondering if my new skirt will show wrinkles. Although I know exactly what Gram means, I say, "I can't help it if you don't like the shape of my face. It's the only one I've got. Besides, I inherited it from you."

The stupid tingling sensation creeps over my body again, and I wish I could be a nicer person. Gram has told me how, when my granddad was alive and really wanted to push her buttons, he'd call her a "narrow-faced woman." Like me, Gram is bony and angular. She's tall, too, for a woman of her generation. She's thin but, unlike me, she has large, heavy breasts. They've sagged over the years, and she is a little stooped. Her face, though lined, is still interesting with its angles and cheekbones. She is definitely not what anyone would call pretty, and probably never was, but there's something arresting, almost aristocratic about her face.

"That's not what I meant," Gram says, "and you know it."

"How do you know what I know? I suppose you know what I'm thinking now too." Why is it I always come to Gram for comfort and then make it so difficult for her to provide it?

"I imagine you're upset because of something your mother said—or *didn't* say."

I don't answer right away. I can hear cars outside, revving their motors at the Dairy Dip down the road, where the older teenagers hang out in the evenings.

"What's *wrong* with her anyway?" I say at last, hating the whine in my voice. "I think she spends more time in that bed than out of it."

"It's never a good idea to judge another person, not when you can't taste their pain."

"How do you know I can't taste her pain? You seem to think you can taste mine."

The smell of Gram's lotion rises from her skin. It's a smell

I associate with comfort. Not sweet, not perfumey, but nice. Cherries and almonds. I'm suddenly sorry for being so obstinate, and I go to Gram and kneel to put my head in her lap. She has a bit of sewing there, and she puts it aside so my head will rest more comfortably. I breathe in the aroma of my grandmother.

The snuff can and spit cup rest beside Gram's chair. As always, Gram has stashed her "toothbrush"—as she calls her snuff dipper—when I enter, but I can smell it on her now, blending with the scent of her lotion. I don't mind the smell—not really—but I abhor the dark-brown liquid visible in the spit cup and the smudge at the corner of her mouth.

Gram strokes my hair. "Now tell me what's wrong."

"I don't know. Everything. Nothing. Nothing and everything." Suddenly I know how my mother feels. The thought leaves me nearly breathless. What if we're the same, Mama and me? What if I'm going to be prone to depression just like her, when there's really nothing to be depressed about? A shudder runs through me; Gram moves a calming hand to my back.

"Sometimes I think she's just making excuses for not living, for not being a real mother," I say.

"You mean faking the headaches?"

I nod, then shake my head. "I don't know. What do you think?"

"I doubt it," Gram says. "I used to have pretty awful headaches myself when I was your mother's age."

"Did you go to bed with them?"

Gram laughs. "No. I couldn't. There was too much to do."

"Did they make you depressed like they do her?"

Gram looks thoughtful. For a second, I think she's going to tell me something dark about herself, which I really don't need to hear just now. Then she shakes off the thought, whatever it was, and says, "I don't think I've been depressed a day in my life. Not like your mother anyway, and I'm thankful for that."

"Oh, Gram." I push away from her and drop back onto the bed, which is getting old and lumpy. "You make me crazy, the way you're always being thankful. If I told you we were all going to die in a blizzard, you'd be thankful because we were going together or something."

Gram's deep-throated chuckle rings out. "Is that so awful?"

"No, but what I don't understand is what makes you that way and her so—so different. And what I want to know is which way am I going to be?"

"Is that what you're worried about?" Gram reaches for her sewing. "Here, could you thread this for me? My old eyes take forever anymore, even with a threader."

I take the needle, thread it quickly, and hand it to Gram. "Maybe you need new glasses. Or maybe you just need to clean the ones you've got." Her old-fashioned cat-eye glasses are mottled with spots.

"Could be." She removes the glasses, spits once on each lens, and shines them idly with the hem of her dress, revealing a few varicose veins on her thighs, and dark-pink indentations on both sides of her nose.

Replacing the glasses, which don't look much better than before, she starts back up with her sewing. When she speaks next, it is without looking at me. "You're nothing like your mother. You don't have to worry."

"How do you know?"

"I just do."

"But . . . I feel so different sometimes. All the time, really."

"Different from what?"

"Different from everybody else or at least everybody my age. Like I think too much or something, like I'm not able to have fun. I know Dad, for one, thinks there's something wrong with me. I think the kids at school do too."

Gram snorts, a small sound of derision. "Here, let me read you something."

She rises and walks over to the small round table on which rests her daily calendar and a small ceramic figure of a dark-haired girl I gave her for Christmas one year when I was little. She limps a little, the way she does when she first wakes up. When she comes back, she has her daily calendar with her. Each

THE TICKET

day she tears off a page, and each day she has a new quote. She shares these quotes with me a lot of days. Today's date looms large—Saturday, September 6, 1975.

I groan though I'm a little curious.

Ignoring me, Gram reads, moving her finger along the words as she does. *The thing that makes you exceptional, if you are at all, is inevitably that which must also make you lonely.*

It is my turn to snort, although it comes out more like a gagging noise. "There's nothing exceptional about me. Who said that anyway?"

"Lorraine Hansberry. She wrote an amazing play called *A Raisin in the Sun*." Gram moves back, a bit heavily, to where she'd been sitting. I've noticed her movements getting slower, less fluid lately, and it disturbs me a little. "And I beg to differ—I think you *are* exceptional."

"If I'm exceptional, it's only in my loneliness. Exceptionally lonely. Isn't *that* special."

"Maybe you just haven't found it yet."

"It?"

"The thing that makes you truly exceptional. I happen to believe you are exceptional and that someday everyone will see it. Even you."

"Yeah, right. Now I know you need new glasses." I snicker, thinking Gram sees me about as clearly as the eye of the needle she couldn't thread. Then I wonder if she has money for new glasses. Gram's skirt is old and faded, like her eyes, which are still a piercing, if pale, blue-gray. I have seen her in this skirt a thousand times. She fastens it at the waist with a large safety pin. I look at it and then away, sort of embarrassed for her, thinking surely she could sew on a button or something, as handy as she is with a needle and thread. Where's her pride?

My chest feels heavy with a sudden insight. I'm always thinking of myself, my wants and needs, clothes for myself—never for my grandmother—while Gram is just the opposite. She's always thinking of someone else. She is the epitome of unselfishness. I cringe at this contrast. I'm probably more like

Mama, no matter what Gram says.

Our family story has it my first word was "Grammy," though I pronounced only the second syllable clearly, and it came out sounding like "me." My grandmother, who could never bear to leave me alone when I cried for more than a minute, was holding me at the time. "It's all right—Grammy's got you," she said. And so Grandma became Grammy and eventually just Gram. Now I wonder if I was already so self-centered that "me" never meant Grammy in the first place.

Yep. Me, me, me.

"Why don't you take up a sport? With your long legs and arms—"

"And total lack of coordination. I'm an embarrassment at sports. You have no idea." I think of all the times I've been chosen last or next to last in gym. So often, I've come to dread it with a passion when our gym teacher tells us to choose teams. I don't know why it should keep hurting every time, but somehow it does.

"You just haven't found the right sport yet. Why don't you try tennis?"

"Tennis?" I think of *Champion's Choice*, one of my favorite books of all time. I can see the graceful champion in the novel dipping low for a difficult shot, wearing a white dress with yellow trim and matching yellow on her socks and hair ribbon. I try to envision myself on the court instead, but the image is too clumsy, too giraffe-like to contemplate.

"Sure, tennis. Long legs and arms are an asset in tennis."

"You mean next summer?"

"No, I mean right now. Why wait?"

"I thought tennis was mostly a summer sport," I protest, the awkward giraffe vivid in my head. "That's when the Rec-League gives classes and all the little kids learn the rules. Besides, I'm probably already too old to start playing."

"Nonsense." Gram pauses and looks at me as though she, too, is seeing me in tennis whites and a sun visor—but probably not as a giraffe. "The thing is—it won't cost a lot to get into it since

THE TICKET

your mom and dad already have rackets around here somewhere. They used to play, you know."

"I know." The thought doesn't help one whit. "Who would I play with? It takes two, doesn't it?"

Gram hesitates. "What about this new friend you went shopping with?"

"Lori?"

Gram nods.

"No way," I say. But a glimmer of possibility shines through, and I add, "I guess I could ask her."

CHAPTER FOUR

"Wake up, Maggie, I think I got something to say to you." I'm startled to hear Gram's aging voice belting the lyrics to one of my favorite Rod Stewart songs. His throaty voice blares out from her radio as I enter, and I realize she's singing along.

I giggle. "What's the deal, Gram? Are you entering your second childhood or what?"

I'm not surprised to find Gram wide awake at such a late hour, sitting in her overstuffed platform rocker, sewing in hand. Like me, Gram is something of a night owl. But I *am* surprised to find her listening to Rod Stewart singing "Maggie May."

"I am not," Gram says, putting her snuff brush aside quickly. "But I couldn't get my station to come in, so I thought I'd try something new. Isn't this one of your singers?"

"My singer," I repeat, liking the sound of that. "You know it is." Since I own only a grand total of four record albums, two of them Rod Stewart, everyone in the house is familiar with the songs. Even Gram has told me to turn the racket off, or down, more than once.

"I laughed at all of your jokes, my love you didn't need to coax. Oh, Maggie, I couldn't have tried any mo-o-ore," Gram sings along, and now I totally crack up. Gram looks indignant, but then she joins in the laughter. When at last we settle down, we sing along in unison to the rest of the song.

THE TICKET

I can barely carry a tune, and Gram's voice, which was probably good once, cracks painfully on the high notes. But we sing together happily, loudly, and exchange grins as the song ends.

"So what are you in such a good humor about?" Gram asks, and I plunk belly first onto her bed. I trace a finger over the swirly, slightly raised designs on the faded brown-and-cream bedspread like I have a thousand times before. Sometimes I see faces in the dashes and swirls, scowling faces or smirking faces, but more often sympathetic ones. Cheerful ones today.

"I took your advice. Lori and I tried out the tennis thing." I prop myself up on my elbows, clasp my hands together, and rest my head on my hands. Gram loves it when I actually follow her advice, especially if it turns out good. Like today.

Gram nods. "And?"

"And it was really fun. You should have seen us. We were awful. We spent most of our time chasing balls we hit over the fence."

Gram chuckles. She has a surprising deep belly chuckle like Santa Claus or some big fat biker dude. "And that was fun?"

"Yeah, it was, actually. And, as bad as I was, Lori was even worse." I grin, thinking of Lori taking an elaborate swing and missing the ball altogether. Not once but several times.

I jump up and demonstrate, feeling only a little guilty about mimicking Lori, until Gram fairly hoots with laughter. "But we got better. By the end, we could sometimes hit back and forth three or four times before we messed up. And there was this man there, watching us, and when I told him it was our first time—like he couldn't have guessed—he said . . ." I pause for a breath, remembering the compliment. "He said I was a natural."

"A natural?" repeats Gram. "Well, well."

I hasten to add, "This isn't one of my stories, Gram. This really happened."

"How did that make Lori feel?"

"Oh, I don't know if she heard him or not. He was on my end of the court. And even if she did, I don't think she'd care. Not that much. She thinks it's funny too when she messes up."

"He said I should take lessons so I'll learn things the right way. He said it's harder to unlearn strokes when you start out wrong than it is to start from scratch. Or something like that." I bend at the knees and demonstrate a powerful forehand swing in what I imagine to be good form. But what do I really know?

"That makes sense, I suppose," Gram says slowly, "but I just don't know how much . . ." Her voice trails off, but I pick up her thought.

"I know, I know." I drop back onto the bed, throw my hands out in front of me, spread my fingers wide and study the narrow, unpolished nails. The fourth fingernail on my right hand is chipped, and I try to even it up with my teeth, though this never works. "Lessons would be way too expensive. I wasn't really seriously thinking I could take lessons. I just thought you'd be interested to know somebody thought I had potential. Somebody besides you, I mean."

Gram looks thoughtful, a little sad. After a moment, her face brightens, and she says, "It's a second-best solution, but maybe you could check out a book on tennis strokes from the library and try to teach yourself the right way. It couldn't hurt, worst-case scenario. And, who knows? It might help." She rolls her sewing up and drops it in the basket at her feet.

Now Linda Ronstadt is crooning, "You're No Good." Two great songs in a row. I sing along while Gram reaches for her bottle of Jergens. She's already in her pajamas, a silky peach pair that have been washed so often they are nearly white. With a small grunt, she pulls up one leg of her pajama bottoms above the knee and smoothes the lotion on her calf, which is thin, but flaccid.

The familiar smell lifts my already high spirits even higher. At this moment, all feels right with my world. "Why is it," I say out loud, "that sometimes you feel like everything is so wrong, and other times you feel like everything is nearly perfect? And things aren't really all that different?"

"I don't know." Gram moves on to the second calf.

"Do you ever feel that way?"

"To a degree, I suppose I do. Though maybe not as extremely as you." She puts the Jergens bottle back on the table.

"Is that bad—to be a person of extremes?" I get up and practice my tennis serve, tossing an imaginary ball high over my head while I wait for her answer.

"Of course not. It just means you have an enhanced capacity."

"For what?" I try a backhand swing.

"For joy."

"And pain," I add softly, letting the imaginary racket fall.

"Perhaps."

"How did you get to be so wise? Were you always like this—like you are now?" I go to Gram and kneel beside her with my head in her lap. Not that I can imagine Gram any different, or that I'd want to, but still I sometimes try to picture her young and foolish like me. I've seen photos, a few old black-and-whites, creased and a little out of focus. In some of them, she's a young, laughing woman. In others, she's a solemn girl, not quite a woman yet. But it always seems like those are pictures of different people, not of my Gram.

Gram laughs deep in her throat, stroking my hair, and the gnarled fingers feel so good, the way they always do. I look up at her and, for a split second, I see the same mouth as in the laughing photos. In the next instant, the familiar face is back—the false teeth and the deep vertical lines etched around the lips. "Not by a long shot. Not that I'm all that wise now," Gram says. "I still do misguided things all the time. I guess I'd like to believe I've learned a few things from my mistakes over the years."

"What mistakes?" When she doesn't answer right away, I stand up and pretend to practice my strokes again. But mainly I'm watching her, because I'm really curious what mistakes she's talking about.

There's a faraway look in Gram's pale blue eyes, and I wonder what she's remembering. "What mistakes?" I repeat.

"With your mother, for one," Gram says. "I wanted so much for her . . . so much for her to feel only the happiness in life, never the pain, that I made it too easy for her. I never demanded anything from her. I tried to shelter her, to do the nasty chores myself, to let her experience only the pleasant parts of life." She shakes her head. "But it doesn't work that way."

"What doesn't?"

"Life. There's always going to be unpleasantness. If you keep a person away from it for too long, they may never learn how to cope. Your mother missed an important lesson." A teardrop blurs one of Gram's eyes, stands there for a slow second before she blinks it away.

I sink back on the bed, trying to think how to make Gram feel better, sorry now that I pushed her to remember painful stuff. Turns out, Gram is not smooth to the core, as I've believed, but may be as ragged inside as me. Like a peach—jagged and prickly at the center and clinging to the last morsels of goodness, as if scared to turn loose.

It occurs to me that I haven't invented a story about my popularity for Gram in some time. Maybe I'm clutching at loose tennis balls, but I think one of my stories might shift her attention from her sad thoughts. I rattle on for a while about the cutest boy in the whole school writing me love poems, which, of course, never happened.

Pretty quickly, though, I can tell the old woman's heart isn't in it, so I give up. And another thing: As much as I love clothes—and I do love them a lot—after playing the game today, I'm starting to realize how much more there is to it than looking good on the court. I was so focused on not missing the ball, I forgot all about looking like a giraffe.

"Do you want me to rub lotion on your back?" I suggest. I rarely offer, though I know how much she likes this; the same way I like it when she strokes my hair.

Gram smiles. "That would be nice."

I pick up the bottle of Jergens, squirt a quarter-sized blob of it into the cup of my palm, and rub my hands together. Nothing worse than cold lotion and cold hands on a warm back, I figure. Gram leans forward. I lift the top of the faded peach pajamas and rub in circles, thinking again of the man at the tennis court. Something in the way he looked at me made me feel funny. Sort of womanly. Of course, he was old and fat and ugly, but someday someone might look at me that way again. Someone who isn't old and fat and ugly. I giggle. "How did you know when you met Grampa he was the one?"

Gram tilts her head, and I know she has the faraway look that always comes over her when she talks about Grampa. "He was the prettiest man I'd ever seen, and there was a gentleness about him I've never known in anyone else. "Loving him was the easiest thing that ever happened to me."

"Men aren't supposed to be pretty," I protest. The men in my novels are never pretty. Handsome or rugged, manly or craggy, but *never* pretty. I concentrate on Gram's right shoulder where I can feel a hard little knot just below the skin, which I try to massage away.

"Well, your grandfather was." Abruptly Gram straightens her shoulders and pats my hand. "That's enough for now. You ought to get some sleep so you'll be fresh for school tomorrow."

I groan, rubbing my hands together to finish off the rest of the Jergens. "You always say that. I can't go to sleep just because it's time for bed. Sometimes I get way too keyed up."

"You can start keying down. Don't ever forget that education is a great opportunity—"

"Not to be squandered," I finish the sentence before Gram can as I edge my way toward the door. I've heard the story hundreds of times—how Gram couldn't go beyond the eighth grade because the nearest high school was too far away, and her parents didn't appreciate the importance of education for a young woman.

"That's right," Gram says, not in the least daunted. "Not to be squandered."

I bring my hands to my face and inhale the scent of lotion. Then I give Gram an exaggerated wink, turn on my heel and walk out the door, even though I know it will be a long time before I sleep. On the way to my bedroom, I hear the front door open and shut. Dad.

On an impulse, I run to greet him, thinking maybe he'll be pleased to hear about me and Lori playing tennis, which is about as far from reading as you can get. And I know—boy, do I know—what a waste of time he thinks reading is.

"Guess what I did today, Dad!" One look at his drawn face and already I regret my decision. How many times has he told me he doesn't like to be confronted the minute he walks through the door?

"What?"

He sounds only a little distracted, so I plunge on. "I played tennis . . . with my new friend Lori."

"Oh?" Dad smiles, picks up the mail that lies atop the foyer table. I'm relieved to see that smile—a tired one, but a smile nonetheless—because I can see the mail is mostly bills, and this usually puts him in a foul mood. "That's terrific. Did you like it?"

I open my mouth to elaborate, but he holds up a hand. "Hold that thought while I go to the bathroom. Okay?"

I practice my tennis swing, eager for him to return. Just as he comes out of the bathroom, though, the phone rings. Figuring the conversation is now officially over, I turn to leave. Dad surprises me by motioning for me to follow him into the kitchen.

I drop into a chair at the kitchen table as he picks up the receiver of the wall phone. I wonder if he's hungry. Perhaps I should make him a sandwich. "You want a sandwich?" I mouth, and he nods okay.

"Should I fry the boloney?" I ask, but he doesn't appear to notice.

"Pee Wee, is that you?" he says into the receiver, his eyebrows twisting toward the bridge of his nose.

I get up and head to the refrigerator, thinking what I'm going to say when he hangs up, and wondering why Pee Wee is calling. Pee Wee Johnson is Uncle Jay-bird's best friend, but he and Dad have never been what you'd call best buddies exactly. Mostly I've run into Pee Wee by accident when he happens to be hanging out at Aunt Sue and Uncle Jay-bird's house. He's a small man, short and slim, with springy hair that stands out around his head

THE TICKET

like one of the three stooges. Uncle Jay-bird is much taller and heavier, so the pair of them makes kind of an odd couple.

"What are you talking about, Pee Wee?"

Something in Dad's voice, an undercurrent of excitement, catches my attention. I listen closely, even as I draw out bologna, cheese, mustard, and mayo, and balance them gingerly while I push the refrigerator door shut with my foot. Dad can't stand it if you leave the door open a second longer than you have to. Wastes electricity.

I decide to fry the bologna since I know he likes it that way. I put the skillet on the eye of the stove and drop just the least little dab of bacon grease into it. There's always a crock of bacon and sausage grease next to the oven to use for seasoning beans and keeping stuff from sticking to the skillet, like when you're frying potatoes. I don't much like the smell of grease myself, but it does make things taste better and cook more smoothly.

"Slow down, Pee Wee, and tell it to me outright, straight and simple." Dad's body is motionless, and I can tell he's hanging on every word being said on the other end. "How much?" he asks, in a funny choked sort of voice. Then, after a pause, "Are you *sure*? Let me write down the details. Hold on a sec."

Dad fumbles with the phone, his eyes darting around until they meet mine. Despite the thinning hair, he is still a good-looking man, with his lean body, chiseled jawline, and bottle-green eyes. For a second, I can see him darting around the tennis court, making unbelievable shots you'd never expect him to reach. The bologna is spattering flecks of grease in my direction now, so I turn down the heat and take the bologna up before it can burn.

Pretending not to have been listening, I resume the sandwich-making process. Mustard on one side, mayonnaise on the other, bologna, and thin slices of cheese, the way he likes it. I decide to spread a little peanut butter on the meat, being careful not to burn my fingers.

But, out of the corner of my eye, I watch Dad. Frantically, he jerks open a drawer, locates a pen and a scrap of paper, and returns to his conversation. He writes carefully, eyebrows still drawn together in a single line. "I don't know about that," he says, the undercurrent of excitement more intense now, though his tone remains even and controlled. "We'll see. We'll have to see."

Pen and paper in hand, he places the receiver gently in its cradle and looks at me. The expression in his eyes tells me he's in no mood for my tennis tale. So I ask, "What did Pee Wee have to say?"

"He says—he says I've won the lottery." Dad's hand is shaking. "Of course it's a mistake, of course, it is. That idiot, Pee Wee. I'm going to wring his neck for putting me through this when I find out . . . how can I find out?" Dad's eyes dart back and forth again, and his shoulders go left as his body goes right, then vice versa. "The ticket. I've got to find the ticket."

I don't know much about lotteries, not enough to understand *exactly* what he's talking about. I've heard him joke about Pee Wee and Uncle Jay-bird wasting their time and money driving all the way to Hazard, Illinois, to buy lottery tickets. Based on that, I'm pretty sure my father wouldn't. What grabs my attention even more than his words, though, is the intensity of his physical reaction. I rapidly finish making the sandwich as he dashes from the room—it's as if his frenzy is somehow contagious.

My thoughts spin. What could this mean? Could we be rich? Rich enough for me to buy some new clothes? The bluish-violet outfit I tried on but couldn't afford flashes in my mind, vivid in details I thought were forgotten—the way the pleats hung just so, the way the sweater felt against my skin, the way it matched perfectly, clinging just enough to be, well, almost alluring.

Dad is back then, frantically waving a ticket and the slip of paper with the carefully written number. "He's not wrong. It looks like, for once in his pea-pickin' life, that goofy little son-of-a-b—son-of-a-gun is *right*." He grabs me and swings me around and around.

I laugh with him—giddy, so giddy—until I'm breathless. I see the outfit still. Periwinkle. "How much did we win, Dad?"

"Enough, enough." Dad releases me and executes a sort of

———————— THE TICKET ————————

rowing maneuver with his hands, revealing so much pent-up energy I fear he may explode. In one breath, he lets out a muffled war whoop while in the next he urges, "Don't tell anyone. Let me think how to do it."

"I won't," I promise. Not only is there a good chance the periwinkle outfit is *mine*, I also get to be privy to a secret with my father. "How did Pee Wee know about it?"

"He bought the ticket. To thank me for giving him and Jaybird a ride that day. He bought the ticket, and he gave it to me." Each sentence is chopped off, spoken as though out of sequence. Jumbled, like his thoughts.

"That was pretty nice of him," I say, absorbing this.

"Yeah, it was. But the thing is—now he thinks he deserves a share. He's demanding his fair share—that's what he said." Dad has gone from excited to agitated in one breath.

"What are you going to do?"

For a second, he looks perplexed, vaguely troubled by the question. "I don't know yet." Then the confusion evaporates, and he turns to me. "I still can't believe I won—I actually *won*. Winning is just something I never expected, not in a million lottery tickets."

I watch the emotions passing through my father's green eyes—amazement, disbelief, something akin to joy. Grabbing my hand, he whirls me into a gleeful dance, spinning and twirling me as I have only seen couples do on American Bandstand. I stumble a little, awkward but pleased.

CHAPTER FIVE

The next day at school, I am dying to share my news. Instinctively, I know this will get a big reaction from my classmates. Keeping silent requires enormous effort, but I manage, telling myself that tomorrow I will be able to tell.

I imagine the scene. The popular kids are all focused on me, their eyes filled with admiration and envy. "What?" they ask in unison. "What did you say?"

"What will you do with all that money?" one of them asks, I haven't thought through which one.

"Will you travel?" asks another.

"Will you move away? Into a mansion?"

"Will you still be our friend?"

The questions pour in, but I am not overwhelmed. To the contrary, I smile benignly upon them all, not reminding them that I was never their friend to begin with.

In my daydream, *I have arrived.*

After school, I can hardly wait to get home to see what kind of dramatic transformation has taken place. Breathless in my excitement, I burst through the front door to find that nothing has changed at all. Dad is at work, as usual. Mama is in her bedroom with a headache, also as usual.

Now I wonder if Dad told her? I have to know. I tap on their bedroom door, brave in my knowledge. "Mama?"

I call twice before my mother's 'I've-got-a-headache' voice tells me to come on in, but quietly. It takes only a few minutes to figure out Mama has not been told. Then I start to worry—could I have imagined the whole thing?

But, no. I remember too clearly. I am certain I did not.

Was Pee Wee mistaken after all? Dad might have forgotten to tell me if he was. Restless with knowledge and uncertainty, I bite back the impulse to confide in Mama. Instead I opt for making the moment more about her, usually the safest strategy with my mother. "How are you feeling?" I ask brightly.

"Not good." Mama presses a hand to her temple. "Would you be a dear and bring me a cool, damp washcloth?"

I bring the cloth and turn to leave. "Don't go." My mother's command comes as a surprise. "Sit down and visit with me for a while."

I perch gingerly on the edge of the bed, trying not to jar the mattress with the weight of my body. The room is dark, which is the way she prefers it when she has one of her headaches.

Still, because I can think of nothing else to say, and because the dark is so depressing *to me*, I ask, "Should I turn on the light?"

"No, no, please." Mama smiles weakly and focuses strained—but still beautiful—deep blue-gray eyes on me. Most of the time, I don't think about Mama's appearance. She's just my mother, as she's always been. But once in a while, when I do—like now—it strikes me afresh how exquisite her features are, even when their beauty is tainted by evidence of pain and pills. "This helps, though. At least for a few minutes." She indicates the washcloth on her forehead.

"I'm glad," I murmur.

"I just get so lonely sometimes, but the effort to talk makes my head throb."

"Do you want me to leave now?"

"No." There's an edge to her voice. "I told you already—no. I want to make the effort. I want to be a good mother to you. You believe me, don't you, Tray?"

I nod. Realizing Mama's eyes are closed now, I say, "Yes."

I am not sure *what* I believe when it comes to Mama's desires as a mother, but I want to please her. And, truly, I want to believe her. In that moment I also sense that she means what she's saying, so, in that moment, I too believe.

"Oh . . ." Mama moans, turning her head from side to side. "If the pain would just go away—everything could be different."

"Do you want me to put some fresh water on the cloth, Mama?"

"No, that's all right." She turns the cloth over, replaces it carefully on her forehead. "I sometimes ask myself what everything would be like if—if the pain went away, if I were different. I worry that it's all my fault."

"What's all your fault?"

"You know—your dad, your Gram . . . you."

"What about Dad? What about *me*?"

"He's so frustrated all the time, and you're so—so unpopular."

Her words strike me like a blow. I want to protest that her description is false—that we're all just fine, and *she* is the only one who's not completely well-adjusted. I want to say Dad *is* satisfied, Gram *is* happy, and I am quite popular. Instead, I find myself mumbling, "How did you . . . know?"

"A mother knows these things." Mama's mouth twists into a new shape, something between a grin and a grimace. "When I was your age, there was more commotion in the house. More friends, more boys." Mama pronounces the word *boys* the way I might say a dirty word, something naughty but also exciting. "In spite of the fact that we lived so far out in the boondocks you practically had to pump in sunlight, and that my daddy was so . . ." Mama breaks off, groans, and presses her forefingers to her temples.

"So *what*?" I am totally curious now.

"So hard on anything that even hinted at the subject of—you know . . ."

I feel my face turning warm. Now I am glad of the dark, so my mother won't notice the blush. In the dim lighting, I can make out the gleam of her eyes, which are wide open, and the outline of her features, the delicate nose, the full, generous mouth. I wonder if she, too, is embarrassed. She has never spoken to me about sex, not even briefly, and I've never been comfortable bringing up the subject. So now, I have no idea where this discussion is heading.

"He embarrassed me so many times. He would threaten the boys that came around, telling them not to touch me, even though we were only friends. Boys who never even thought about touching me in the first place." She pauses, sighs. "At least that's what I thought back then."

I'm still uncomfortable, but also spellbound, trying to imagine Mama as an embarrassed young girl. "That must have been awful for you."

"He always said boys just have one thing on their minds. I thought he was crazy, but later it turned out he wasn't so far off as I thought." Mama's eyes droop shut again. "I was pretty naïve. And when my daddy warned me like that, I didn't know what to think. I only knew one thing for sure: I knew Daddy loved me. Even when I'd get so mad at him, all I could think about was getting away, deep down, I knew he loved me. I've never been quite that certain about anyone else."

"What about Gram?" What about me? *I* love you.

Her eyes flutter open, and she seems startled to see me, as if she's been talking to herself. "Of course your grandmother. I meant anyone of the opposite sex."

"What about Dad?" My heart thuds like crazy at the secrets my mother is telling. For the first time, revealing pieces of herself I've never known. I am thrilled by all this instant camaraderie, even though I know how she is. Capable of saying things one day and forgetting them totally by the next.

Still, I have to defend Dad because, even if I sometimes doubt his love for me, I never doubt his love for Mama. Everyone knows how much Jesse adores Evelyn. The way he looks at her, the way he pleads with her—when he thinks I'm out of earshot—and I'm wishing I were too—*to come to bed, to let him kiss her, do things to her*. What things exactly I have only a foggy idea about.

"My father always said a boy will tell you he's in love with you when what he really means is that he's in *lust* with you," she says to me. To *me*, as if she's reading my mind. My face grows really hot. I want to go to my room, put on a record album, and forget this conversation. I rise to leave.

"Don't go. I didn't mean to upset you." Mama sighs. "I didn't mean your father was like that. I just meant . . . you can see why I was so mixed up back then. It's no wonder I couldn't be a real wife, the way Jesse wanted. I just meant it's not my fault."

Her face contorts as if she's about to crumple into tears, and I find myself longing to comfort her the way a mother would console her child. It's not the first time she's made me feel like this.

I sink again on the bed, careful not to shake it.

"It's okay, Mama. I understand," I say although I certainly do not.

She sighs and I know the moment is over. I shouldn't have bothered to sit. "I need to be alone now," she says. "But could you freshen my cloth once more before you go?"

I take the cloth and escape to the bathroom, relieved at the respite from too much information. I run the water for a few seconds to make sure it's as cold as it will get. I place the cloth under the gush from the old faucet, wring it free of excess. When I return to her bedside, Mama is lying so still, for a moment I think she's sleeping. But then the blue-veined eyelids flutter, and a languid hand reaches for the cloth.

Just as I pull the bedroom door closed, I hear a noise at the front door. The familiar pattern of my father's footsteps announces his arrival, unexpectedly early today. I rush to meet him, bursting with our shared secret, the conversation with my mother all but forgotten.

His eyes are bright, and he grins at me. "You haven't told anyone, have you?"

I shake my head. "Are you going to tell Mama?"

"I think I should. Don't you?"

I nod, pleased to be the first to know, and pleased to be asked for my opinion. I wonder how she will react. She'll be glad. Surely

THE TICKET

she will be glad. "Tell her now," I urge.

Already, Dad is moving away from me, his stride a curious blend of determination and uncertainty.

"Do you want me to come with you, Dad?"

For a second I think he hasn't heard. Then he pauses and, without turning to look at me, he says, "No. Thanks."

I am disappointed, tempted to listen at the door. But I know both he and Mama frown on eavesdropping in a big way. To resist, I hurry to my own room and put a favorite record on the turntable. I turn the volume up loud enough so I'll hear nothing from my parents' bedroom.

CHAPTER SIX

I CAN'T BEAR it any longer; I've got to see how thrilled Mama is at the news. I step into the hallway just as Dad comes out of the bedroom. He smiles at me, but it's a funny sort of smile and I can't read its meaning.

"Is she glad?" I say. "Is she excited?"

"You might say that," he answers, the odd smile still hovering around his mouth. "Yes, excited is the word."

"Can I tell Gram now?"

"Sure. Why not?"

I yield to a sudden impulse to see Mama before going to Gram. Mama and I have never been close, not like Gram and me, but I'm thinking—hoping, after our surprising conversation today —maybe that is about to change. Dad left the door open, so I step cautiously inside to find Mama frantically pushing through the clothes in her closet, tossing garments into a heap on the floor.

"What are you doing, Mama?"

"None of these will do. I'll need to buy all new clothes now. But surely there's *something* here I can wear." She jerks items from their hangers as though infuriated by their presence.

"There's nothing. Nothing at all," she whimpers, sinking into the pile on the floor and dropping her head onto her hands.

I touch her shoulder tentatively. "Are you okay?"

THE TICKET

Her eyes dart in my direction, like a bird seeking sustenance. She rises, says almost gaily, "Of course I am. Why wouldn't I be?"

"You just seem—sort of different."

"Different's good, isn't it?"

She takes my hand and asks, "Do you know how to jitterbug?"

I shake my head. "What's that?"

"It's a dance, silly. I'll show you."

Amazed at this woman who just moments ago writhed in bed with a headache, I watch as she releases my hand and executes a dance step with an invisible partner, her face—with its pale, flawless skin, short straight nose, brilliant blue-gray eyes—so animated, her movements fluid and graceful. "Now, you try." She reaches a hand toward mine. I take it with misgiving.

I know even before I try that I cannot do this. My movements are jerky, and I can sense Mama's tension mounting when I consistently move in the wrong direction.

"Never mind." She drops my hand abruptly. "You can learn later. There's time for you. It's not too late."

"Too late for what?"

"Come here." She drops onto the bed and gestures for me to join her there. She lowers her voice. "You know about the money, don't you?"

I nod, relieved she is talking sensibly now.

"Well, *money is the key*. When we didn't have it, I never told you that because I didn't want you to be sad. But now that we do, you should know."

"Know what?" *The key to what?*

"With money, you can get what you want." Mama's gaze on me is fevered, and I think of Gram. Gram would not approve of this attitude, but maybe Gram is wrong. *Maybe* my mother is right.

"What do you mean?"

Mama's eyes peer past me, into the distance, as if she is seeing someone else, someone not in the room. "There was this boy once and he cheated on me. I didn't know why at the time. I kept asking myself what she had that I didn't have. I thought it was about looks or charm or personality. We were young, so young, and yet he knew. Even then, he knew."

"Knew what?"

"He knew about money, and eventually he married this girl, a girl whose family *had money.*"

In a few short minutes, Mama's taken me from joyful to astonished to troubled. I can't help feeling a little sorry to learn Mama was hurt, even so many years ago. But mainly I'm angry at her for talking this way about someone who is not my dad. What disturbs me most of all is the intensity of her tone. It's like this boy was the love of her life. I stiffen at the implications for our family. And especially for Dad. For Jesse, who loves Evelyn *so much.*

"It's too late for me," she goes on in a conspiratorial way, as though we are in the habit of sharing such secrets, and perhaps we are. Perhaps now we are. "But it's not too late for you."

"Too late for what?"

"To get your Donnie."

THE TICKET

CHAPTER SEVEN

Paradise, Kentucky
July 1969

Perhaps I always knew there was something different about my mother or perhaps not. Maybe there was an instant when realization dawned though I can't remember such a time. I try to think back . . . back to myself at twelve, at ten, at eight . . . *You're driving me crazy*, she'd say, or *I'm as nervous as a cat*, and, especially, *You're giving me a pounding headache*.

Often Dad scolded me too. *Can't you see you're getting on your mother's nerves?* At other times, he apologized for her behavior. *She doesn't mean to*, he'd say, or, *She can't help herself,* after my face was slapped for spilling a drink or leaving a toy where she might trip over it.

The apologies helped a little, but they also confused me. Without them, I might have assumed the fault was fully mine and the slap rightly deserved. Dad's explanations created doubts in my mind. Was it possible my mother was to blame somehow?

But, no, Dad's point was that Mama was not to blame, not ever, no matter what. Sometimes it seemed to me there were two Evelyns, or maybe three. The one who was so wrapped up in her headaches and her daydreams, she barely acknowledged my existence; the one who truly wanted to be my mother—or at least my friend; and the third Evelyn—the frightening Evelyn, who appeared rarely. This Evelyn was the one I tried not to think about.

Mostly it was the self-absorbed Evelyn who lived in our house.

When the second Evelyn appeared, the one who loved me, she could turn on such charm and gaiety that, for a brief moment, I'd feel like the most special girl in the world. For long stretches of time, the nice Evelyn, the real Mama, emerged only in my memories. But even my memories were mixed up because sometimes the nice Evelyn was the most loving and charming just before the frightening Evelyn emerged.

When I was eight, Grampa died. We'd been staying with Grammy and Grampa in their creaky old farmhouse for some time—a few months probably, though it felt like years to me. I loved being with Grammy, and I usually loved being with Grampa, too, but now he was so very, very sick, and it wasn't the same as before. I missed being at home, where my toys were and a neighborhood gang of kids I sometimes played with back then, before they became too cool for me. Worse were the constant admonishments to be quiet because Grampa was trying to rest. Grampa had something called "cancer." I wasn't exactly sure what cancer was, but I envisioned it as sort of like a fast-growing giant wart, only on the inside instead of the outside.

Grampa's room was at the top of the stairs, and sometimes I'd go bounding up before I remembered. He lay there in bed with a pained expression in his blue eyes, his sandy hair slick with sweat, and his reddish freckles standing out against his pale, pale skin—which was usually so reddish-brown from the sun you could hardly see the freckles at all. Still, he'd try to smile when he saw me. Every time I'd forget how sick he was and let out a squeal or bounce a ball in the house, someone heard and shushed me. It was worse, even than Mama's headaches, which hadn't gotten quite so bad at that time.

Being reprimanded, I'd feel guilty, knowing how my Grampa loved me and how sick he was. I loved him too—of course I did! I was his little angel, wasn't I?—but he'd been sick *forever*, it seemed to me. Sometimes I wanted to be young and carefree and *loud*.

Then Grampa died, and there was even more whispering and shushing than before. There were phone calls to be made, and more food in the house—people from neighboring farms kept tapping on the door and dropping off dishes. They'd pat me on the head, saying, "Bless your little heart" or "You poor thing!"

One lady in a flowered dress and black hat said, "How your Grampa loved you. He thought you hung the moon." This startled me, because the other thing that was happening the day after Grampa died was that "man" walked on the moon. The "man's" name was Neil Armstrong, and this was happening on television and everybody was talking about it, when they weren't telling us how sorry they were. They'd get all excited talking about the man on the moon, and then remember and get serious again.

"How your Grampa would have loved to see this," Grammy said. "I just wish he could have lasted a little longer—if he hadn't been in so much pain."

Outside, I stared up at the moon, which looked exactly the same as before. I thought I saw some shadows in it, though, and I asked Dad: "Is that him? Is that Neil Armstrong?"

"No," he said, laughing a little. "You can't see him from here."

I didn't know what to think. It made about as much sense to me as a man in the sky playing hopscotch on the stars. After that, I would mix up the two events: Grampa dying and Neil Armstrong walking on the moon. It was as though Grampa had taken a new form on his way to heaven, and he was the one walking on the moon.

Grammy was very upset. Usually, no matter what happened in the family, she was the one I could count on to find the funny side. Not this time. Her nose was red and dripping all the time, though I didn't see her cry except once. When she saw me, she dried her eyes quickly and apologized. "I'm sorry. I'm just being selfish because—because—I'm not myself," she said. "You'll have to overlook your Grammy's foolishness."

That was just it: *She wasn't herself*. Nobody was. I was no longer sure who I was either. I'd gotten so used to being the center of Grammy and Grampa's world before he took sick, but now I had the feeling I'd never be the center of anybody's world ever again, though I couldn't have put it into those words at the time.

Everyone sang praises for Evelyn's calm, her poise, her gracious handling of the funeral arrangements, the visitation at the funeral home, and other things I didn't understand. But by the day of the funeral, she began to behave strangely.

I watched her from out of the corner of my eye during the service. I knew I should be feeling sad about losing my grandfather, but mostly I felt scared about what was happening to my mother.

My ankle itched inside my stiff lace-trimmed sock. I bent down to scratch it and, when I came back up, I glanced over at my mother. She had the strangest expression on her face, like she was hiding a giggle.

In the days following the funeral, Mama bubbled with pent-up energy, like a teapot about to reach the boiling point. There was an odd feeling in the air—a certain tenseness in Grammy's expression, a peculiarity in the things Mama said, a worried look in Dad's eyes. Then, one day, about a week after the funeral, the strangeness reached new heights.

As I was dressing for school, Mama appeared abruptly in the doorway of my bedroom. "What would you like to do today?" she asked.

A glint of wildness in her eyes should have alerted me, but her words were so welcome, I ignored the warning. "Uh . . . I guess I have to go to school."

A tinkling laugh told me I was being silly. "Shall we play dress-up? Would you like to wear my pearls?"

"What about school?"

"Pfft!" Mama waved a hand dismissively. "School will always be there. Besides, you have a good excuse."

I nodded, not sure if the excuse was my grandfather's death or something else clear only to my mother. I loved Mama's clothes, and playing dress-up was one of my favorite pastimes.

On dozens of occasions, I'd pleaded with Mama to play with me, or let me try on her grown-up clothes. I learned that she was virtually *never* in the mood. After an endless string of "not now" or "not today" responses, I had quit asking.

For Mama to bring the subject up herself not only astonished but totally delighted me. It was as if she had invited me to fly to Paris with her. Or the moon.

I swallowed my concern and gratefully allowed her to brush my hair, piling and pinning it on top of my head like a grown-up. Together, we rummaged through the closet until she saw me staring at a cream-colored dress draped with tiers of matching lace and adorned with a narrow blue satin sash.

"Here!" she announced. "This one's perfect for you."

Taking care not to wrinkle or soil the dress, I eased into the delicate fabric. The dress was too big, but I felt glorious. I twirled and twirled until Mama motioned for me to stand still while she tied the blue satin sash.

Suddenly she glanced at the clock on the nightstand and gasped. "What are we doing? You've got to go to school! Quick—get out of that dress and get going. I don't know what your teacher will think of me. I can't imagine how I let you talk me into this. How many times do I have to tell you that being a mother means making tough calls? It means *saying no*. What sort of excuse can I write for you? Oh, oh . . . I just don't know what to do anymore."

I fought the impulse to deny having instigated anything. I wanted to defend myself but, even more than that, I wanted to console my mother. "It's all right," I said. "Mrs. Jacobs is cool. She won't say much."

"Don't just stand there. Get out of that dress this instant. You can't wear it to school. You look foolish."

Crushed, I obliged.

When I came home from school that afternoon, my nose cringed at a sharp acrid smell. "What's burning?" I called out.

"My hand," Mama said. "How did you know?"

Sure enough, the side of Mama's hand was fiery red, as though she had laid it directly on a burner.

THE TICKET

"Mama!" I said. "That looks awful. It must hurt like . . ."

"Hurt?" Mama laughed as if I'd told a funny joke, not that she ever appreciated any of my jokes. Or Dad's either, for that matter. "You don't know what hurt is."

"You better get something on it. Medicine or something. Did you hold it under the cold water tap?" She gave me such an odd look, I explained, "That's what you always tell me to do."

Now, it seemed, I'd become the adult in the family, my mother the child in need of care. "Here, let me help," I said.

I reached for my mother's arm and led her toward the kitchen sink. I caught sight of a bright red burner on the stove top and a skillet of scorched beans. Without releasing Mama's arm, I turned the burner off and moved toward the sink, reaching to turn on the cold water.

Just as I brought her burned hand under the cool stream, Mama jerked abruptly away. "Did you hear something?"

"No, I don't think so. Like what?" I tried to keep my voice calm, despite the wild eyes being turned on me.

"Quick—run—hide in the closet! It might be your father."

"*What?*"

"Now is no time to ask questions. Just do as I say. *Get in the closet!*" she gritted, pushing me toward the kitchen doorway so hard I lost my balance and fell.

I scrambled back to my feet.

"*Hurry.*" Her voice was urgent.

"Which closet?"

"Which closet, which closet . . . It doesn't matter. The coat closet, for heaven's sake."

I ran to the closet in the front hallway and pushed aside the coats to huddle, shivering . . . wondering and waiting, in the dark, in the quiet. For what, for how long, I have no idea. Eventually, when I was wondering if I should come out, wondering if Mama had forgotten where I was, I heard a sound and eased the sliding closet doors open to peer out.

A door was opening. My father's deep voice rang out near the back door. "Evelyn? Are you home?"

A scream echoed through the house. Like the sound of an animal being tortured or slaughtered, it was both my mother's and not my mother's. "Don't touch me, you beast!"

The voice ripped, splitting open at the soul, like the cracks that had appeared in the concrete driveway to our house. And now it was my mother herself who was cracking wide open. How she hated those cracks in the driveway, always saying, "We've got to do something about those nasty cracks," time and again. How then would she be able to stand the weeds springing from her own brain?

My mother is crazy, I thought, and then, maybe it isn't Mama who is crazy. Maybe it is me. What am I *doing* huddled behind these stupid coats?

I slowly slid the closet door open a bit more and took a tentative step outside. My mother's voice was shrill. "I know what you're trying to do, sneaking home at this hour. Don't think I don't know. You can't fool a fool, you know."

My father's deeper, quieter tone came then. "What is it you think I'm trying to do?"

"You're killing me, aren't you? You're murdering me a little at a time. Or is today the day to finish the job?" She rushed into my view with my dad trailing hesitantly behind. I crouched back into the closet like a coward but left the door open. Like a person drawn to an accident, I had to see what would happen next. "Don't come near me, I'm warning you," I heard Mama scream.

"Okay, okay." He lifted his hands as if to ward off blows.

"I mean it. I'm warning you: If you take so much as a single step toward me, I'll—" Mama had moved back into my path of vision now, and I could see her clearly from where I huddled. A grotesque snarl distorted my mother's beautiful face into something unspeakable.

Shifting my weight on legs that had started to tremble, I summoned the courage to leave my hiding place. But before I could force motion into my quivering limbs, my mother seemed to sense my presence. She swept me fiercely into her arms, rushed me with amazing strength from the hallway, up the stairs to my bedroom. "Your father is planning to kill us both," she explained in urgent, hushed tones. "Run to the Chalmers' house across the street. Fast, *don't look back.* You've got to go now, and maybe you'll survive. Now *go!*"

"But . . ."

"There's no time to argue." She grabbed my shoulders and shook me so violently my teeth banged together. "Don't you hear what I'm telling you?"

I nodded.

"Then go! Now!" She pushed me back toward the stairs. For an instant, I thought she was going to push me down the steps as well.

I ran breathlessly down the staircase and out the front door, my thoughts spinning out of control. What would I say when I reached the neighbor's? That my mother was stark raving mad? I wondered if Mama could be right, if we were both caught in a crime drama where the person you thought you knew turned out to be someone altogether different.

Could my father be evil?

No. No, no, no . . . it was Mama. I knew it was. Not that she was evil exactly, but something was not right. I glanced back to catch sight of her on the front porch, waving me on, motioning frantically. "Never look back," she called. "It's bad luck. Remember the Bible."

For a second, staring back at her, I froze. And, in that moment and for a long time after that in my memory, my mother's wild eyes and disheveled clothing froze, too—into a blurry statue of translucent granules—like Lot's wife in the Bible.

CHAPTER EIGHT

LATER THAT SAME year, when I was eight and a half, I awoke on Thanksgiving morning to a world of white glistening, swirling snowflakes piled in soft heaps on the ground, clinging in dazzling array to tree limbs and still falling, drifting, the flakes large and luminous. Each one unique, I'd learned in school. How was that possible, I pondered, when they looked so much the same? Did we human beings look as much the same from a distance? If there was life on another planet, or on the moon—of course, I knew there wasn't, or at least Neil Armstrong hadn't seen any—but if there *were*, and if that life could see us on earth, would we all look exactly the same, the way ants and snowflakes look to us?

I stuck out my tongue to taste the snow once I was outside. It didn't have much taste, and yet it was glorious. I corrected myself. It *would* have been glorious if only . . . if only my mother were there to see it. Not that Mama particularly appreciated the beauties of nature. Dad was always trying to get her to admire the colors of the birds or trees, but she didn't have much use for stuff like that. She was more likely to see the spots on the carpet, the puddles on the floor from dripping boots or shoes. Still, her absence left a gaping hole, like the missing front tooth I had only recently begun to replace with a jagged new growth.

I was one of the last kids in my class to lose my baby teeth—despite being one of the tallest—and I had relished the ache of

THE TICKET

wiggling the baby tooth back and forth. The old tooth, the baby tooth, would never return. I wanted to cry for its loss. As I ran my tongue over the rough edge of the newborn tooth that took its place, a sudden fear seized me that my mother's departure might also prove permanent. One couldn't replace a mother. You could never grow a new one.

The aromas of Thanksgiving greeted me at Mimi and Paw-paw's house. We always spent Thanksgiving with Dad's family rather than with Grammy, even before Grampa died, and Grammy became someone not quite herself, and Mama . . . well, I didn't know exactly what was going on with Mama, but it wasn't good. The smells were good ones—sweet apple cider, baking turkey and bread and pies—and my stomach growled hungrily. This I felt must be a betrayal of Mama, and so I punched myself in the belly to shush it.

A gust of cold air announced the arrival of each newcomer—aunts, uncles, cousins, just about everyone from Dad's side of the family (which was way bigger than Mama's, who was an only child. Most of Gram's brothers and sisters had died or moved off up north). They called out gaily, all the while stomping off their shoes at the door, slipping out of their scarves and coats and hats.

"Can't remember the last time we had a snow like this on Thanksgiving," Uncle Jay-bird said, and a chorus of voices tried to recall. Everybody acted so normal, like nothing had changed. No one mentioned Mama at all—it was as though she had never existed.

I remembered—not the exact year, not even my own age at the time—just Mama's voice in the car on the way to Mimi and Paw-paw's singing. *"Over the meadow and through the woods, to Grandmother's house we go. The horse knows the way to carry the sleigh through the white and drifting sno-ow!"* Mama's voice was pure and sweet, like a bird. She wasn't singing for herself. She was singing for me. After all, it was *my* grandmother's house, not Mama's. A hot tear broke loose and splashed onto my cheek at the memory. I wiped it away with a fist before anyone could see.

"Let's eat," Mimi announced. Everyone gravitated to the

table with murmurs of appreciation for the plentiful spread of vegetables, of turkey stuffed with cornmeal dressing, and the bowl of gravy, topped with slices of boiled eggs.

Although my stomach continued to growl, the food on my plate held no appeal, so I just stabbed at it with my fork. The conversation swirled around me as the snow had swirled around me outside. Uncle Jay-bird was telling a joke, something about a man going to a doctor with a problem. I didn't think it was funny, but then, I wasn't really paying attention. It was probably one of those jokes Mama wouldn't have laughed at either.

My father laughed loudly, though. "I've got one," he said.

I can't believe he's telling a joke, I thought, and then his words caught my attention. "You know the story about Lot?" he said. I could see my mother's surreal image as she hastened me, cautioning me not to look back. My breath caught in my throat while I waited for Dad to continue with his joke-telling, waited for the punch line. "Well, the part you don't always hear is *why* his wife looked back—after the Lord had warned them about what would happen if they did, you know."

I froze altogether; not a muscle moved. Had he heard and seen the same thing I had that day? Somehow, my breath eked out, little by little, still waiting. "The thing you don't always hear is what Lot said to her right before she looked back. He said, 'Do you think we're being followed?'"

For a second, no one laughed, and then they did. Not uproariously, but politely. Were they as shocked as I? Were they all thinking, as I was, of Evelyn and what had happened to her?

Why would he tell such a joke?

I started breathing again, forced a smile, remembered in that moment how certain my mother had been that Dad was out to harm her, to harm us both. *Was there any chance she'd been right?*

No one spoke my mother's name that day, or my grandfather's. No one told me how sorry they were, as everyone had at the funeral home and after the funeral. It was as though I had dreamed the whole thing, as though Grampa had never existed either, any more than Mama.

THE TICKET

Maybe I was invisible too.

I pushed my plate away. I thought of a painting I saw once of a bunch of farm animals sitting around a table. Now I saw myself as a sad-eyed dog, surrounded by cats, wolves, monkeys, pigs. How disgusting we all were. Aunt Sue with her long skinny neck was a giraffe. Zoo animals, caged animals, but they weren't the ones caged. It was Mama who was caged. Caged in an asylum.

What was an asylum anyway? I wanted to know, but at the same time, I was afraid of knowing. I hated the images that haunted me when I closed my eyes.

"What do you want for Christmas?" Aunt Sue said, and I realized she was talking to me.

"I dunno."

"Haven't had time to think about it yet?" My aunt looked sympathetic, and for a second, I was touched.

I remembered then, something I once overheard Mama say about Aunt Sue. "I don't know why your sister doesn't like me," she'd said.

"Why do you say that?" Dad sounded puzzled.

"You know it's true. Everything I do is wrong. I can't even wash dishes to please her. The last time I did, I caught her rewashing the ones I'd already finished."

"That's ridiculous."

"It certainly is!" Mama had snapped back.

So I shrugged at the question. I'd been waiting, I realized, for someone to speak of my mother, to ask about her. I held my breath to see if Aunt Sue might say her name. *Where's your mom today? How's your mama? What do you hear from Evelyn?* But she didn't.

Did they not know? Not care? Could they have simply forgotten her?

They had not seen what I saw, or they could not have forgotten. From the Chalmers' house that day, I watched the car coming with lights blinking, the men in blue forcing Mama into the backseat, Mama kicking and screaming, Dad looking on with the saddest expression you ever saw. *How could you ever forget something like that?*

Later, when Aunt Sue was passing around the chipped blue bowl containing folded slips of paper for our Christmas gift exchange, I caught my breath again. Would there be a slip of paper with Evelyn's name on it? Surely there was . . . but what if there wasn't?

I wanted to ask Dad, but he was deep in conversation with Uncle Jay-bird. Something about Wildcat basketball it sounded like. Always one of their favorite topics. I watched Dad closely. I thought he looked distracted, the smile forced, but I couldn't be certain. He was speaking now, motioning with his hands. Uncle Jay-bird nodded, picked his teeth with a wooden toothpick. I turned away, nearly bumping into Aunt Sue.

Aunt Sue's hands were empty. I stared at them, thinking there should be an extra name, the one for my mother. "You okay, honey?"

Clutching my slip of paper, I hesitated for a second, and then the words rushed out. "Did you give Mama's to Dad?"

Aunt Sue looked blank for a moment, but the vertical line between her eyes deepened. "I didn't do one for your mother, I'm afraid. I didn't know how long—I mean—I didn't know if she'd be here for Christmas or . . ."

Not be here for Christmas? My worst fears were justified—they were writing Mama off. It could just as easily be me someday, hauled away by men in blue and written off as if I'd never lived. I dropped the wadded slip of paper—the name on it unread—and rushed past Aunt Sue, through the door to the cold snow outside, not stopping to put on my over-boots or my coat. Not stopping for anything.

"Tray!" someone called after me.

I ignored the voice, ignored them all, and fled. I was crying when I reached the car and climbed inside, not knowing where else to go. Crying for myself, crying for my mother. *Someone* needed to cry for Evelyn, and there was nobody else to do it. Nobody but me.

Maybe I was afraid—afraid to have fun with my cousins,

afraid to play, afraid I too might forget. It was up to me to keep my mother alive.

I wasn't surprised when Dad flung open the car door. I knew I'd wanted him to follow me, even though I had nothing to say to him. "What's the matter with you?" he demanded. He was carrying my coat, and he placed it awkwardly around my shoulders.

"You don't understand," I said through my tears. "Nobody does."

He said nothing, but he squeezed my hand and somehow I knew he did understand . . . I knew he was hurting, too.

He just hid it better than I did.

The day Mama came home from the asylum was both the best and the worst day of my life so far. I had awaited her return so anxiously, determined to make up for all my past failings as a daughter. I would be the ideal child, neat and obedient, focused and helpful. Gone would be the piles of dirty clothes, the water splattered on the bathroom mirror. Even my posture would be perfect, which would probably require constant effort. But I would make that effort gladly until holding my shoulders back, and my stomach in, came naturally. I would avoid mud puddles. I would take my shoes off and clean them before tracking dirt clods onto the carpets. I would shine the faucets every single time I used them. If having a daughter who didn't constantly disappoint her could keep my mother well, she would be gloriously well.

I skipped up the stairs and down again to get the house ready. Up and down, up and down, I took the stairs two at a time as my mind darted ahead of my body. I changed the sheets, plumped the pillows, shined the mirrors, placed a vase of flowers in Mama's bedroom. But then, in an anxiety attack, I worried it might leave a circle on the dresser. I searched for just the right item to place under the vase. Not a potholder—not in the bedroom. A lace cloth, but that too might circle. Finally, I settled for drying the bottom of the vase ever so carefully, and placing it on a cut-glass coaster.

Grammy laughed at my efforts. "Your mama may not be in any state to appreciate all that, Tray-bien."

"What do you mean? She's fixed, isn't she? Or she wouldn't be coming home."

Grammy smiled, but there was something strained in the smile. "Yes, I suppose so. But she may have other things on her mind."

"Like what?"

I wondered what Mama could have on her mind, what she had *ever* had on her mind. I didn't know, could not imagine. Perhaps I had never really cared before, or not cared enough.

I decided to make Mama a special dinner with all of my favorite foods because I was not really sure what Mama's were. I resolved to find out, to prepare her favorites in a day or two. I sang, *"Over the meadow and through the woods . . ."* as I worked, envisioning my mother's pleased surprise. It would be like a late Thanksgiving celebration. "When did you learn to do all this? I had no idea my little girl was growing into such a talented cook," she would say. "This is really delicious. What did you put in it?"

"A real chef never gives out her recipe," I would say. "Chef" was a new word for me, one I couldn't wait to surprise Mama with by using correctly. "There's always a secret ingredient." And we would laugh together in delight, with me promising to share the recipe since I was so glad to have my mother home.

But when Mama arrived, she was not hungry. She barely glanced at the elaborately set table, the chocolate pudding that wasn't the instant kind, or the spaghetti with meat sauce that didn't come from a can.

I was deflated. I fixed myself a plate of food. Grammy joined me, trying to cheer me up, and we pretended it didn't matter. My mother—her daughter—was home, after all. That was what mattered. I laughed loudly at her jokes, moving the food around my plate and winding spaghetti on my fork. It kept slipping off, and I tried to think of a joke to crack about this. But my heart wasn't in it, and after a time Gram gave up, too. It was during this meal that I began to call her Gram instead of Grammy. Somehow

THE TICKET

Grammy just sounded so babyish all of a sudden. We cleaned up the kitchen together without much conversation. Still, the knowledge of Mama's presence in the house reassured me that at least one wrong had been righted.

Later that night, I bounced down the stairs in search of my favorite doll, Sally. Mama and Dad were talking, and their words stopped me cold about halfway down. There was something in my mother's voice, sharp and clear and altogether frightening. I had the chilly feeling I didn't know this woman at all, this woman who had given me life, and I wondered if Dad was feeling the same way.

"They said you might take it this way. You might not really want me to get completely well because if I ever did, you wouldn't even know me and I might not even *like* you." Evelyn's voice rang with accusation. I shivered, not knowing if getting completely well was something my mother had already achieved or something she was still working toward.

I crouched on a step, longing to escape back up the stairs to my bedroom, but unable to move. I waited for my father's answer. "I want you to be well more than anything. If anyone doesn't . . ."

"You're going to say it's Mother. Go ahead and try to blame it on her, like you always do. I know what you think." A smirk entered my mother's voice, if it's possible for a voice to smirk. "You think she coddles me too much, and likes to keep me dependent on her. And you may be right, heaven knows. She may not want me well either, because if I became that other person, who knows if I'd belong in either of your lives?" She laughed—an odd, mirthless laugh.

"Did you notice all the preparations Tray made for your homecoming?"

"Mmm."

"She's becoming such a lovely girl, don't you think?" I cocked my head a little, surprised Dad had noticed my preparations and pleased by the compliment. But I tensed to hear my mother's reply.

"I've never thought Tray a pretty child," she said coldly, and her tone spoke so clearly of the utter worthlessness of all my efforts. Pretty, the thing I lacked, the thing I had zero control over, the one measure of worth in my mother's eyes. The backs of my eyes stung with the tears I held in. I welcomed the rough texture of the carpet under my bare legs, abrasive to my ugly skin. I was thankful for the dim lighting that would keep my ugliness from glaring too sharply if my parents' eyes turned suddenly on me, as they were likely to at any moment.

I swallowed down my sobs, swallowed hard, but a hiccup escaped. Their heads whipped around in my direction.

"Tray, is that you?" It was Dad's voice, full of concern for what I might or might not have overheard. On his face, a stricken look; on Mama's, nothing.

I froze, watched as a look passed between them. I saw Evelyn turn on her charm, as palpably as one might turn on a television set. Dad hesitated, then succumbed as my mother spoke, dismissing me. "See you in the morning, sweetheart."

Released, I found I was able to rise on legs that trembled only a little. I was surprised I still had the strength—fearful I might have had to crawl instead. I dashed to my bedroom, slammed the door, and flung my awkward nine-year-old body—already growing too long for my years—onto the bed, where I cried against my pillow and my worn stuffed bear, Jack, with his little button eyes—eyes that never judged or found me lacking. I thought of my doll, Sally, hoped she wasn't feeling neglected where I'd left her.

My tears poured out, bathing me and Jack in a pool of sorrow. My mother might be crazy, but she had beauty and charm. I had neither. And then, just as one despairing thought slipped in and settled, another one followed: what if I, too, sprouted the seeds of insanity?

The next day, when I awoke to sunshine, my spirits lifted a little, in spite of everything. Perhaps, after all, it was a relief not to have to work so hard to please my mother, since nothing I had done the night before had been enough. Never enough.

My efforts, I knew then, would always fall short.

THE TICKET

CHAPTER NINE

Paradise, Kentucky
September 1975

EXHILARATED FROM MY evening on the tennis court, I bound toward Gram's room. It is such a perfect fall evening, cool and sweet. I carry my racket—Mama's racket actually—and take a swing, narrowly missing a vase on the table in the hallway.

I was hitting the ball so well today. It feels so right when all the elements come together the way they sometimes do. I'm getting better, I just know it. Still, I have such a long way to go. A couple of older teenagers at the courts tonight, a dating couple, grabbed my attention for a long time. They hit the ball so beautifully with long, smooth strokes. The girl wore a crisp white tennis dress, and the boy wore immaculate beige shorts and a yellow shirt. They were like something out of a dream, a dream I long to live one day.

I stop abruptly, hearing unexpected voices coming from Gram's room.

"It's been one request after another, ever since I came into that lottery money. Everybody wants something. Everybody has a need, or a cause, or a demand." The voice is Dad's.

"I was only thinking of you and your family," Gram says. *Your family?* Since when am I not Gram's own family? "You know

THE TICKET

you'd rather have me out of here."

"That's not true."

We would *not*, I want to shriek.

"Now's your chance . . . and you can't say you can't afford it."

"Don't tell me what I can or can't afford. You have no idea what my commitments are, what I need to spend or invest—for the family."

"You're right, of course," Gram says, so softly that I can barely hear. "I have no idea."

"What about Tray? You know how much she depends on you."

"Maybe Evelyn would do better if I were gone. Maybe she would become a real mother to Tray. Tray needs her. I won't be here forever."

The fear that Gram might actually leave squeezes at my chest so tightly I can barely breathe. What would I do without her? I cannot hold back any longer. I rush into the room. The sweet nut-like aroma of Gram's lotion assails my nostrils, and I shudder at the thought of losing this comfort, this constant source of strength.

I burst into the room, startling them both. "Don't say that!" I cry, flinging my body onto Gram's lap. "Don't go. *Please* don't go. I couldn't bear it."

"How long have you been listening?" Dad demands.

I'm sobbing into Gram's skirt. Gram retrieves her sewing, her needle and thimble, and places them in her sewing basket so she can stroke my head. "Answer your father," she instructs.

"Long enough," I say, my voice muffled.

"There, there, child, don't cry. Don't much look like I'm going anywhere."

Dad turns to leave, glancing back one time at me and Gram.

When he is gone, Gram tells me to straighten up and talk to her, to stop chewing my thumbnail into the quick. She asks the question I've heard from those wrinkled lips a thousand times, but which today inexplicably threatens to bring a stream of fresh tears, "Have you had anything to eat?"

"I'm not hungry," I manage. "I had three cans of pop when I

finished playing."

"That's not very nutritious," Gram scolds. "How was your game today?"

"Not bad," I brighten, but only a moment. "Don't try to change the subject, Gram."

"What subject?"

"Why do you want to leave me?"

"You might be better off without me, Tray. Sometimes a crutch keeps a person from healing."

"Am I sick?"

"That's not what I meant."

"You mean Mama, don't you? She's the one that's sick."

"Maybe," Gram says. "Besides, even if I was to leave—and I'm not saying I am—I'd always be with you."

"You're not making any sense. How can you be with me if you're not with me?"

Gram lifts a blue-veined hand and presses it first to her own chest and then to mine. "In here. When you've loved someone for so long, they become a part of you. You take them with you wherever you go."

"So you *are* leaving!" I pull away.

"I didn't say that. Let's not cross any bridges until we get to them," Gram says. She loves using old expressions like that—almost as much as she loves sharing her calendar's thought of the day—and I don't tell her that my English teacher calls them clichés. Then she adds, "It doesn't look as if anything much is going to change around here."

"But what if—Dad could change his mind, and . . ."

"What did I just say?"

"I know, I know."

"Some things are meant to be, and some things aren't, so there's not much point in worrying. All things work together for those who love God, you know." Gram reaches for her worn Bible, and I know without being told that this quote comes from there.

THE TICKET

"*Guess what? My dad won the lottery!*" I have at last been allowed to share the news at school.

We are in math class, but the teacher hasn't arrived yet, and the class is buzzing. I'd expected them to rally to the announcement, but I'm not quite prepared for the scale of their reaction. With these few words, I find myself the center of attention in a way that's never happened before. Not like the attention I get when I say something stupid or square, which is way too often. Heads spin in my direction, and some of the kids address me while others talk to each other *about me.*

"What?"
"Get out of here"
"You're kidding!"
"How much?"
"You're lying!"
"How much?"
"Are you serious?"
"What did she say?"
"How much did he win?"
"*She said her dad won the lottery!*"
"Wow! How lucky can you get?"
"How much is he going to net?"

I am embarrassed to admit I know few details, so I pretend I'm not allowed to divulge. This is a good strategy, I think, holding me at center stage, which makes me kind of happy and kind of uneasy at the same time. Like I've invented the whole thing, and it's only a matter of time till I'm busted.

"Oh, come on. Tell us," says Rodney Irvine, a cute boy with red hair and freckles. He reminds me of Richie Cunningham on *Happy Days*. Inside my head, I sometimes call him "Rod." Like my favorite singer. Besides, Rod is a much nicer name than Rodney—it suits him better too.

"Who's to know? We won't tell," urges Brian Tate. Brian is a chubby, but popular boy who is Rodney's best friend.

"I'm sorry. I can't. Really." I would have succumbed, I suspect, if I had the answers. I don't even know if Dad has gotten the money yet. I have to fight the urge to blurt out this additional ignorance.

I stretch my legs into the aisle, admiring my new red knee socks and wishing my legs were a little curvier and not so long. The socks are made of a nice stretchy fabric, so they don't sag around my ankles. I wonder if I should have bought black or white instead. I'm limited in what I can wear with the red ones, and I doubt if I can wheedle my way into another pair so soon.

I flex my ankle to watch the way the fabric clings. Things are going to be different now. I am going to be different. Boys are talking to me, begging me for information. I see what I have not seen before, what my mother tried to tell me. Money is power. And if I don't have any, which I don't, at least they think I do.

Or will soon.

"So does your dad buy lottery tickets all the time?" Rodney asks. I hesitate, then shrug, not knowing if Dad has ever actually bought a lottery ticket at all. I think of Pee Wee Johnson, who does buy tickets, including the winning one. I can't be sure from Rodney's tone whether he thinks buying lottery tickets is cool or stupid. Is he jealous or scornful?

"What would you do with the money if you won it?" Brian asks. He's speaking to Rodney, not to me. I'm all ears for the answer, though.

"First I'd buy a car. A sweet Corvette. Then I'd probably invest the rest," Rodney says. "The stock market or something. Wouldn't you?"

"No way," Brian snorts. "You can't take it with you, you know. I'd buy a big ole yacht, the biggest one I could find."

"I'd buy a mansion with an indoor swimming pool so we could use it all year round," says Adam Whittinghill. He's a tall, angular boy whose family is supposedly rich. Adam's family has a pool in the back yard. It's cold today, though, and will be for several months. I figure his pool is probably drained for the season.

"How old do you have to be to buy a lottery ticket anyway?"

THE TICKET

Rodney looks at me as though I am a fount of knowledge on the subject, and I flush a little just to have his eyes on me.

"I don't know," I admit.

"Eighteen probably," Adam says.

"I doubt it," Brian disagrees. "If you've got the money, I don't see why anyone would care how old you are."

"Some of us could save up our money and go in together and buy a bunch of tickets." Daniel Brown, who is pale and pretty quiet most of the time, joins eagerly into the conversation.

"You have to go to Illinois to get it, right? Because there's no lottery in Kentucky. Not yet anyway," Rodney says to me. He leans in my direction, and I catch a whiff of something salty and masculine. I wonder if he has just come from gym class.

I notice the looks being cast in our direction from several girls in the class. My best friend, Lori, glances our way too, a curious expression on her face. "I *think* you have to go to Hazard, Illinois," I say to Rodney. "That's where it came from."

"I'm pretty sure you're right," Rodney says. "If your dad goes there all the time, maybe some of us could go with him next time and—"

Mr. Ross has arrived and is rapping on his desk. "*Attention, please.*" He raises his voice, sounding exasperated. I am glad for the interruption, grateful this is one question I won't have to answer. This much I know: Dad does not make regular lottery ticket trips and, even if he did, he wouldn't welcome any of my classmates tagging along. For a second, I wonder if there's any chance I could talk him into it?

I try to focus on Mr. Ross's words, but he might as well be pantomiming an opera for all that registers with me. My mind keeps replaying the conversation; most of these boys have never said a dozen words to me.

As much as I tell myself I scorn girls who flirt, the truth is, I wish I knew how. The way it works, not only so I could flirt if I ever wanted to, but so I'd at least recognize when it was being done to me. I'm not altogether sure about what just happened. Could they have been flirting with me? I don't think so. No, they were just interested in learning about the lottery. But still . . . it's an opportunity, but only if I can think of something clever or funny to say.

"Clear the books off your desks," Mr. Ross announces, "and get out a clean sheet of paper."

Oh, crap; a pop quiz. The class groans. I haven't been listening, and now I'm about to be penalized. Mr. Ross writes some problems on the board, and I manage to solve most of them. Rita Davis, who sits behind me, hisses in my direction. I try to ignore her, but the *pssst* is so loud and persistent, I worry that Mr. Ross will hear it before Rita gives up.

"Just move over in your seat a little so I can see your paper, Tray," Rita says. "Come on, please . . ."

Rita's parents run a fashionable dress shop in town. I know this, although I have never been inside the shop. Intrigued by the clothes in the window, I asked my mother once if we could go inside.

"We could," Evelyn said, "but there's not much point. We can't afford anything in there, and I, for one, am not in the mood to be snubbed."

"I can get you a good discount on clothes," Rita whispers now. "Better than a discount. I could get them for you at cost."

I wonder how cheap that would be, then slide over a bit in my seat.

"A little more to the right. That's good. Thanks."

A pang of conscience strikes, and I know I will never follow up on Rita's offer. I would be too embarrassed to admit to being bribed. Gram would be so ashamed. Still, I don't move back until Mr. Ross starts down our aisle to collect the papers. Rita didn't even invite me to her party, I remember, wanting to kick myself for being weak and stupid. Two popular girls from the class, Candy and Poppy, call to me as we file out into the hallway. "Say, you want to do something together—you know, maybe this weekend?" Poppy asks, while Candy stares in my direction. I'm sure they were among those whose eyes were on me earlier while the boys were talking about lotteries.

Still, I'm shocked. I find my tongue. "Sure, I guess. Okay."

Lori is ahead of us. She looks over her shoulder, and I meet her eyes for a second before turning back to Poppy. "I mean, that would be great."

"Good. I'll call you, okay?" Poppy flashes a big smile. She and Candy saunter off.

My heart races. I look ahead to where Lori had been a minute ago. She is gone, but the odd expression in her eyes lingers in my mind—uneasy, unhappy, or something. Then, with a jolt, I know what it was. She looked disgusted. *Disgusted by me.*

CHAPTER TEN

I'm browsing through the refrigerator, the way you would a library with a disappointing collection, when the phone jangles. I snatch it up, hoping it's for me. Of course, it isn't.

"For you," I holler to Mama from the door to her bedroom. "It's about the lottery money."

"What?" On her feet in an instant, Mama grabs a robe and dashes into the kitchen.

"A camera crew's coming!" she announces when she hangs up, untying her robe and tossing it onto the floor. "To film us when we get the check." She lunges back to her bedroom and into her closet, where she starts pulling dresses off the hangers. "What can I wear? What can I possibly wear?" She turns to face Gram, who is in the process of straightening Mama's bed. "This place is such a mess—we've got to get it spotless by tomorrow. Tell me what to do, and I'll do it."

"I could really use some help with the vacuum—," Gram begins. Quick as a flash, Mama has torn from the room to retrieve the vacuum cleaner before Gram can even finish her sentence.

Mama's mania mounts through the following day as we anxiously await the arrival of the check and the camera crew. Racing from room to room, she wants it all to be perfect. Of course, it is not. Too many people live here for one thing, and, for another, lots of our stuff is getting old and faded or cracked.

I try to help, but it seems like I'm just in her way. I plop onto my bed, and she rushes in behind me.

"Don't lie on that bed!" she shrieks.

"Where do you want me?" I say. She's really starting to worry me.

"I don't know—I can't think—Why can't you help me instead of getting in the way?"

Because you're out of control, I think but don't say. Instead, "Help you how?"

Mama looks at me like she's seeing me—really seeing me—for the first time in years.

"You can't possibly wear that," she says, and I look down. More than an inch of ankle shows beneath the slacks I've clearly outgrown, and the buttons on my blouse look as if they might slip from the buttonholes at any moment. *I keep telling you I need clothes*, I think, but again do not say.

Mama frantically rips through the meager selection in my closet. "Is that it? Is that all the clothes you have?"

"I've been trying to tell you." I can't resist this time.

She pulls a fuzzy yellow sweater and plaid skirt from a hanger. "Here. Try this."

"I thought you hated that outfit," I protest.

"When did I say that? I don't even remember when you bought it."

"The day I bought it. You said the color was all wrong for me."

"Well, it probably is. But you've got to wear something."

Mama points to a faint glimmer on the ceiling of the dark closet. "What's *that*?"

"That's my stars. Remember how I wanted to put them over my bed when I was little, and you wouldn't let me? You said they were too tacky, so I put them in the closet instead."

"Oh, my God!" she screams. "I said they were tacky because they *are* tacky. They've got to come off. Now. Quick. Get me a chair."

I drag a chair to the closet and Mama climbs onto it, picking at the old stickers. They will not budge. She scratches and scratches at the edges futilely. In exasperation, she makes her fist into a sort of paw and claws away at one star until the star is shredded and, behind it, the off-white paint of the ceiling has chipped away as well. A dark gaping hole like a goblin mouth leers at us from the ceiling. Mama stuffs her fist into her mouth and gasps.

"Don't, Mama," I beg.

My mother opens her hand and shows her fingernails to me. They are broken, and one is bleeding. She sinks from the chair into a heap on the floor, sobbing. "What can we do?"

"But, Mama, nobody's going to be looking in the closets."

"I am. I am." She sobs harder.

Gram appears in the doorway, and she speaks firmly. "Try to pull yourself together," she says to Mama. "They will probably just go in the living room."

"Who? Who?" Mama stares at Gram now as if she's the villain in a horror film. "What have you done?" she demands, jumping to her feet.

"I haven't done anything," Gram says gently.

"I'll say you haven't," Mama mutters, unfairly I think. After all, it's always Gram who does the majority of the work without much help from Mama on any normal day.

And then they are here. Around us, cameras are being positioned on tripods, and men in khaki trousers or jeans and pull-over sweaters are talking about lighting. "Can we open these curtains a bit?" one of them asks Mama.

"Certainly," she says, and I'm surprised by the calm self-possession in Mama's voice. Maybe it's going to be okay, I think. But then I catch her staring at her face in the mirror beside the china cabinet. She drops the forced smile abruptly, but there is something in the mask of stillness beneath that frightens me more than ever.

I cannot take my eyes off my mother. I'm frozen—the way you are in those nightmares where you really need to act or run but you can't move at all—while I watch Mama grab the arm of one of the younger men. He's looking through the lens of his camera, though not in Mama's direction. Through clenched teeth, she tells him, "I'm ready for my close-up, Mr. DeMille," and she looks like she's about to die laughing at something she's just thought of.

"What do you think about all this?" someone on the camera crew asks. I pull my eyes from my mother's troublesome expression to meet his gaze. He is sort of cute, about twenty or thereabouts, sandy hair, friendly brown eyes, and an eager to please expression. Like a puppy. For a moment, I wonder what he means. Is he asking what I think about winning the lottery or about my crazy family?

Before I can answer, my attention is drawn by a sudden shift, a stillness in the room. All the cameras point at Dad. An older gentleman with a pointed beard and bushy white eyebrows hands him an enormous check, bigger than the posters I sometimes do for school. Surely this is a joke. You can't go to the bank with a check that size, can you?

Dad takes the check, smiles a broad, strained smile, and glances in the direction of Mama, who lunges toward him at lightning speed.

An explosion of flashes from cameras illuminates him like an angel about to ascend, and then Mama snatches the check and giggles. "I'll take that," she says.

Another flash of light and I realize that, outside, actual lightning is adding to the effect.

"What are you going to do with the money?" Puppy Eyes asks me. He does not have a camera, though he has some sort of device hooked to a belt around his waist.

"I don't think that's up to me to decide," I say, thinking of the new clothes I am longing for and of my one pair of new socks. But, maybe, now that we really have the money . . . *maybe* things will be different.

Mama, holding the gigantic check, now postures for the cameraman. I am *mortified*. What will the kids at school think of this fiasco? Gram stands quietly out of the way, and I shoot her a nervous but grateful smile. Why can't my family act normal for even one day?

Another flash of lightning and the door rattles. Everyone looks in its direction. Pee Wee Johnson stands there, hands on hips, dripping with rain. He wears cowboy boots, and a Stetson hat replaces his usual baseball cap. A crackle of thunder supplies the only thing needed to make the ridiculous show complete. My eyes drop to Pee Wee's hip, where I'm half expecting to see a holster and gun. "I'm the one what bought that ticket," he says.

A corner of my brain registers that his grammar isn't usually so bad. Or is it? Maybe he's posturing for the camera, too? Silence falls, and the cameras point once more at Jesse. "Is that true?"

Dad hesitates for just an instant before nodding.

The cameramen glance at each other. Then a tall man in a tee-shirt and jeans makes a brief motion with his forefinger. At this signal, they all move toward Pee Wee. Quickly. As if capturing an action sequence in a war zone. One of them asks Pee Wee, "Tell us—tell us everything."

Pee Wee talks, his expression a little smug. I notice, as I have not noticed before, that he speaks with a strong southern twang. There's no question now: we will all surely come across as a bunch of loony hicks. Longing to escape to my room, I instead remain frozen in place, listening to Pee Wee's story. It has the ring of truth.

"See, I always buy the numbers from my mother's birthday for myself," he explains. "Usually my buddy Jay-bird drives me and him to Hazard, Illinois, to buy our tickets. But Jay-bird's car was in the shop, so we asked Jesse—he's Jay-bird's brother-in-law—to drive us over. I don't drive m'self. A lousy couple of tickets and they'll take your license away, you know? Anyway, riding my bike keeps me fit. To make a long story short, ole Jesse said okay, he'd give us a lift. But when we git there, Jesse says he'll just sit in the car. He don't even want to go in and buy a ticket. Are you sure, I ask him, not believin' my ears. He says he is, he don't believe in throwin' his money away on no lottery ticket. So to thank him an' all, I bought him a ticket. But for Jesse's ticket, I just changed one number on my mother's birthday, making her a year younger as it were. So when I heard the winnin' number

THE TICKET

announced, I knew right off it was the one I bought. So I called ole Jesse right away—he never would-a even knowed he won if I hadn't, not bein' a lottery man hisself—and I told him the good news. I ain't thinkin' he believed me at first. But I just told him, like I'm a-telling all of you out there in television land . . . I only want a little share."

Pee Wee pauses and looks imploringly from one cameraman to another. "It's only fair," he says. "Don't you agree?"

Okay, I have to admit it does sound fair. Mama lets out a small sound, her mouth round. I'm not sure, but I think it is the word "no"—or maybe it's "oh." Her face is about to crumple into tears, and the cameras are all over her now. The cameramen are intent, but there is a hidden smile in their busyness. They are eating this up.

I move quickly to Mama's side, taking her arm and pulling her out of the line of flashing cameras. "Excuse us, please," I mutter. Then, with as much dignity as I can muster—not just for me, but for Mama too—I escort her from the room.

CHAPTER ELEVEN

I'm expecting a fight, but Mama surprises me. She's pretty docile as I lead her away from the scene in the living room. I think she too is relieved to have escaped. She sinks onto her bed without undressing, and smiles wanly at me. Her eyes are kind of glassy, though, like she's not quite sure what's going on.

I'm still reeling from the experience myself, and I'm wondering if I dare leave her alone or if she'll head back into the living room to create another scene. "Do you need anything? A glass of water?" I suggest.

She motions to her bedside table, and I see that she already has a glass of water. She slips her shoes off and collapses onto the bed with a groan. With an effort, I manage to get her under the covers and sort of tuck her in. She groans again and closes her eyes.

After I leave Mama alone in her bedroom, I can hear the camera crew loading up their equipment. Pee Wee has gone, too, and I wonder if everyone else feels as let down as I do. I've got to think that if this is the peak of winning the lottery, it's not such a big deal after all. Maybe they won't even air the segment. I *hope* they won't.

One of Gram's quotes comes to mind. From Ecclesiastes, I think. Something about money and vanity—it is like chasing the wind. *Chasing the wind.* I wonder if my dream of fitting in with

THE TICKET

the popular kids is like that. Still, I have to try, don't I?

And what if I could catch the wind? Wouldn't that be fabulous? My heart beats faster at the mere possibility. Even as I tell myself it wouldn't be all that great—not really—my body thinks otherwise.

I stare at myself in the dresser mirror. Of course, my face *would* choose this weekend to break out something fierce. I dab medicated acne cream on the spots, crinkling my nose as I always do at the stinky smell. I flop onto the bed, where my math book lies open to tonight's assignment. The overhead light in my room is so dim I have to strain to see the page. Do lights go out in stages, I wonder.

I unplug the gooseneck lamp perched on the corner desk and feel behind my bed for the outlet. Finding it, I plug in the lamp, which I balance precariously on the bed. But when I flop down beside the lamp, it falls over onto its side like an uncoordinated bird. I sigh. I can't remember if the cord will reach if I put the lamp on the bookcase headboard of the bed, so I try it.

Barely. I reposition the angle of the neck to direct it toward my book. But even with the light, I can't concentrate. Pretty soon, a series of meaningless doodles fills my paper while the first problem stays unsolved. I tell myself not to think about Poppy's call—about why she hasn't called yet, or when she might call, or what she will say if she does call. Time drags.

When the phone finally rings, I jump to answer, pulse racing, thankful for the extension in my bedroom, a Christmas gift from Mama and Dad a couple of years ago. It's the only one in the house except for the main phone downstairs in the kitchen.

"Hello?" I try not to sound overly eager.

"Hey, how's it going?" Just Lori. My heart slows.

"Fine." I hope Lori won't keep the line tied up too long. If Poppy calls and gets a busy signal, will she keep trying? Maybe, but I don't want to take any chances.

"You don't sound fine."

"Yeah, I'm okay. My face is breaking out though. Wouldn't you know it?" So stupid, I think, as soon as the words are out of my mouth. Of course Lori doesn't know about my plans—or hopes—for the weekend, and I've got the distinct feeling that confiding in her now—though I'm tempted to do so—would not be a hot idea.

"What do you mean?"

"Nothing." Will I ever be able to persuade Dad to part with some money for clothes, I'm wondering—or for going out with Poppy and Candy? Or did I dream that whole conversation?

"What are you up to?"

"Nothing really, except—" Lori hesitates. "It's my mother..."

"What do you mean?" Lori doesn't know how lucky she is. At least her mother isn't as crazy as a Betsy bug.

"It's so embarrassing. It's getting so that every time we go inside a store, I'm expecting our name to be on a list, and half the time it is."

"That's awful," I say, and I mean it. "I'm so sorry." But still not half as embarrassing as what people will say when they see the check being presented to my crazy family. I'm hoping more than ever that the tape never airs or, if it does, that it will be at a time when nobody is watching. What if Poppy sees it? What if she's trying to call right now and getting a busy signal?

"And my *dad*," Lori goes on. "He gets into such a rage when he finds out." She lowers her voice. "Last night he punched a hole in the door to their bedroom."

I am shocked by this. I can't imagine my dad doing anything like that. He would probably be too worried about the cost of fixing it.

"How does he find out?" I ask.

"Different ways. Sometimes people call the house, you know, because we owe them money. And sometimes it's when he gets the stuff from the bank and sees that the money's all gone. I think that's the worst."

"Yeah, that stinks." I do not want to be rude, not when Lori needs me to confide in. I really do feel bad for her, and I want to be there for her. But I have so much other stuff on my mind right now. I am dying to pour out the whole story of the check

THE TICKET

presentation, but I know it will take forever once I get started.

"Hey... wanna come over?" Lori sounds hopeful but a little uncertain.

I realize it would be better than waiting for a call that never comes, but I don't want to take a chance on missing the call either. "I can't," I say, and then I blurt out the first excuse that pops to mind. "I'm trying to get my homework out of the way tonight."

"On Saturday?" Lori's voice is incredulous. "Why?"

I am stumped. There is something so uncharacteristic about doing assignments for Monday any sooner than Sunday night that my mind, like Lori's, refuses to take the effort seriously. Which explains why my paper is basically blank. "Why not?" I say, best I can come up with.

"No reason, I suppose." Lori pauses, and I wonder what she is thinking. "Well, I guess I'll let you go then."

"Okay. Bye." I hang up, torn between relief and guilt.

I'm such an idiot. Nobody's going to call. I try to concentrate on my homework. When that fails, I decide to polish my nails. I suck in the biting aroma of the polish. I like this smell so much better than that acne stuff. I turn my stereo on, smudging the polish a tad. As always, my spirits rise a little at the sound of Rod Stewart's scratchy voice. Even when the lyrics are sad. I rub the polish off the smudged nail and reapply it, humming along to *Reason to Believe.*

The lyrics make me think of Rodney Irvine—Rod Irvine to me, though I've never once heard anyone call him that. Maybe his name is one of the reasons I like him so much. I drift into a fantasy in which Rod is totally crazy about me. "I don't know what it is about Tray," he says to Brian Tate. "But somebody like that makes it easy to give." He looks at his friend, his eyes wide with his love for me, perplexed by his inability to control his feelings.

I laugh aloud, the fantasy fades. How ludicrous—I have about as much chance of having Rod *Stewart* crazy about me as I do of Rod Irvine. I will never fit in with the popular kids. I am too uncool.

Okay, so I figure I should call Lori back. I reach for the phone, but another voice inside intervenes. *If you are to have any chance at all,* the voice says, *you have to take advantage of whatever opportunities come along. Like now. You cannot afford to worry about loyalty to Lori. Loyalty is weakness,* the voice hisses. I say the words aloud. I like the taste of them, although they bring a shiver, the same one I get whenever I say something hateful to anybody. I imagine them written on Gram's calendar of the day, with my name in italics as the person given credit for the quote.

A frown puckers Gram's face at finding my name on the calendar. *"Loyalty is weakness?"* Her voice is sad. "I don't think so, Tray."

I push the thought of Gram away, think of my mother instead. "Money is power," I say aloud.

I suddenly feel chilly and jump off the bed to pull a sweater from the closet. The sweater is long and droopy, the result of having hung in the closet all summer. I know you're supposed to store sweaters in drawers, not on hangers, but I forgot. Besides, I like it long and droopy. Better, at least, than the ones where the sleeves are too short. Which is most of the stuff in my closet.

Pulling on the sleeves so they completely cover my hands, I can almost hear Evelyn's voice warning, "Don't do that. You're going to destroy the shape of that sweater forever." I stare again at myself in the mirror, wishing for the ten-thousandth time I was pretty. Pretty is power, I think, but I do not say it aloud. Maybe, just maybe, *money* is more powerful than pretty. Money is *real* power.

I drop back onto the bed and write in a mathematical notation: *Money > Beauty.* I like that. I will never be pretty, but I might be rich some day. I might even be rich *now.* So I decide I will ask Dad about new clothes.

And, while I'm at it, I will ask him to turn the heat up in the house. He has this thing about keeping the temperature warm in summer and cool in winter to save on electric bills. But now, with the lottery money, he is bound to change. I'm sure he just hasn't thought of it yet. He hasn't adjusted to our new circumstances.

THE TICKET

It's up to me to tell him, and, while I'm at it, I'll definitely ask for some new clothes.

I know he is in the house somewhere and don't want to wait another minute. I hop from the bed, grab a clean sheet of paper and jot a few figures down, prices from the catalog. I compare the sum to the amount on the big check, and my hope soars. Even if he doesn't get to keep it all—he's been complaining about taxes or something—the total for the clothes is so small by comparison.

I can't wait to show him.

I hang on to the seeds of hope as I locate Dad at his desk in the den. I open the catalog to one of my favorite pages for him to see. The tall model—she's a brunette, like most of my favorites—is wearing an elegant off-white pantsuit. Her long hair falls gracefully over one shoulder, wavy but not at all frizzy, and her eyebrows are arched and delicate. But mostly what draw me in are her clothes and accessories. The pant legs flare gradually, and she wears very high-heeled strappy black sandals and holds a black clutch in one hand. The jacket has three-quarter sleeves and a single button. She wears it open over a blood red top with a chunky silver bracelet on one wrist and no other jewelry. Simple sophistication, the very image I long to cultivate.

Despite the expression on Dad's face, which is not exactly encouraging, I compare the figures I've scribbled for a couple of outfits to the amount of the lottery win, to help him see the light. He grabs the catalog and throws it onto the floor. "*This again?*"

"But I thought . . ."

"You and everybody else."

"What do you mean?"

"I mean that if I gave in to every request that has come my way, I'd be in the poorhouse by now."

"So you're not giving in to any of them?" I demand. "Not even your own family?" I remember what Brian Tate said about how you can't take it with you. These words hold a new ring of truth for me now. *You can't take it with you, Dad*, I want to say. But I only ask, "So what *are* we going to do with the money?"

"You just don't understand how complicated it is."

"How complicated *what* is?" I notice that Dad's pants and shirt, like mine, aren't exactly brand new—the cuffs are a little frayed if you look closely, and the fabric of the trousers is faintly shiny, though that could just be the light. But at least they fit.

"Having money."

"Why is it complicated?" I think of Lori and her family. I think that not having money is complicated, too. Which is worse? Surely *not* having money is worse.

"If we don't *plan* how we're going to use it, if we just start spending on this and that and the other, it will disappear in a flash, and we'll be wondering where it all went," he tells me, snapping his fingers to illustrate his point.

"But, Dad, I really *need* some new clothes."

"Have you heard anything I just said?" He looks directly at me; something flashes in his eyes.

The phone rings and my need for clothes evaporates for the moment. I rush to the kitchen and grab the telephone. "Hello?"

"Is Tray there?" It's Poppy. She sounds breathless, and I hear someone giggling in the background.

"Just a minute." I cover the receiver with my hand. "It's for me," I call to Dad. "I'll just take it in my room. Could you hang it up for me?"

I tap my foot while he saunters into the kitchen to take the receiver. The second it touches his hand, I bolt to my room, where Rod Stewart croons *Every Picture Tells a Story*. I jerk the needle off the record, so as not to miss a beat of this conversation. Also, Rod might not be considered altogether cool by Poppy and her crowd. I wish I had a Led Zeppelin album to put on instead.

"This is Tray," I say, and my voice cracks a little.

THE TICKET

CHAPTER TWELVE

THEY ROLL OUT of the car, the three of them, bubbling with laughter. The redhead Poppy, perky and curvy, though she's only a year older than me, fairly sparkles with delight. Leslie, who's slim and darkly sensual and whose boyfriend is driving the car, joins in with a throaty chuckle. Candy—plainer with brownish-blonde hair, the one I feel the most hope of connecting with—laughs just a shade too loudly.

My heart lurches with hope at the possibility of being a part of this fun-loving crowd. I've waited a whole week for this opportunity, alternating between excitement and dread-tinged hope. When Poppy called the first time, it had been only to tell me they had other plans.

"Next weekend," she'd said. "Next weekend we'll do something."

As it turned out, only a few of the kids at school had actually seen the check being presented—enough, though, to generate discussion. To my relief, no one mentioned my mother's odd behavior. Instead, they focused on Pee Wee Johnson.

"*Did that guy really buy the ticket?*"
"*Are you going to give him some of the money?*"
"*Would you?*"
"I would."
"*No way! It's tough luck, but a gift's a gift.*"

THE TICKET

As before, the guys spoke more to one another than to me.

I glanced at Poppy, who was watching and listening. I couldn't read her expression. I didn't feel friendly vibes exactly, but interest at least. I forced a smile in her direction.

"I'll call you," Poppy mouthed.

I believed her at the time, but as the weekend droned on, and I stayed near the phone, I only ended up wondering why Poppy was leading me on. I'd just about given up hope when the second call came.

"Sure, I'm free," I said, heart thudding.

"We'll be there in a few minutes. Be sure to get some money."

"I'll try."

And I did try, stopping just short of pleading. But I was unable to get any cash on such short notice.

Now, face-to-face with these popular kids, I am flooded with nervous excitement. The accompanying sense of dread that I will mess it up somehow is so strong, so convincing, it nearly dashes the spark of joy, leaves me more uneasy than thrilled, which is what I want to be. Why do I have to overthink everything—what is wrong with me anyway?

"So you got any money?" Poppy demands without preamble as the car pulls away from our driveway.

"Not much," I admit.

"How much is not much?"

Embarrassed, I open my purse and self-consciously count out my change. Even my handbag looks square and old-fashioned beside the other girls' blue denim and bamboo bags. "A dollar and some change. I guess about two dollars total."

Poppy snorts her disgust.

"Is that all?" Candy says. "Even I have more than that, and my dad didn't win any lottery."

I can think of nothing to say. I sit stiffly in the backseat, next to the door. I turn slightly away from Candy, who is in the middle, to press my forehead into the glass.

Leslie, in the front seat beside Steve, turns around now with a look of annoyance. I cringe before realizing the annoyance is directed more at Candy than at me. "It's not her fault if her dad won't give her any of the money," she says.

"I don't know," Candy says, a hint of defensiveness in her rebuttal. "Did she ask him? How do we know if she asked him?"

"Look, I told her on the phone to try and get some money," Poppy says. They are discussing me as if I am not here.

My lip starts to tremble, and I stare at my lap so no one will notice if I cry. Next to Candy's, my legs look awful. They are too long and, instead of curving into the car seat, they angle bonily, knobbily above it. I wish I'd worn jeans instead of my denim skirt so I wouldn't have to look at them now. There's a small hole in my tights right on top of my left knee. I pick at it nervously. Candy's legs, in contrast, are petite and sexy in hip-hugger bell-bottoms.

I have an inspiration. When I get home, I will split the legs of my best jeans, and Gram can sew an insert into each leg to convert them into gigantic bell bottoms. To escape the present conversation, I picture the jeans, see myself in them instead of this ridiculous skirt and tights. But I waffle between envisioning a bright red bandana for a bold contrast, or a less conspicuous blue fabric for the insert.

"Didn't I tell you?" Poppy says. No one answers for a moment, and then I realize she's talking to me.

"What?"

"Didn't I tell you to try to get some money for tonight?"

"Yes, I did try. But . . . but my dad wasn't home."

"When's he going to be there?" Poppy demands.

"I don't know. He works late a lot."

Poppy snorts. "Well, I don't see why. If I had all that dough, I'd never work again."

"Yeah, well . . . my dad's kind of different."

"So where to?" Steve wants to know.

"Let's go on to the bowling alley like we planned," Leslie says.

"Maybe by the time we bowl a game or two, her dad'll be home and she can get some cash," says Candy.

"I doubt it," I mumble.

"If we didn't know better, we might think you didn't want to ask him," Poppy says.

"Let it go," Leslie says. "Let's just have some fun."

"Sure, sure, fun," agrees Poppy. Poppy's jeans have ragged holes in the knees, and the bits of leg showing through the holes manage somehow to look curvaceous. Remembering all my hope and anticipation and excitement about tonight, I suddenly hate her. After way too much agonizing over what to wear, I could scarcely have chosen worse if I'd tried. Not that I own anything like Poppy's brown leather boots or Candy's fringed suede jacket anyway.

A few minutes later we're inside the bowling alley, and the girls are mumbling together again and hooting with laughter. I can't even understand what they're saying, but I try to laugh along, my face feeling stiff and strained.

"What are you laughing about?" Poppy turns on me suddenly.

I don't want to admit I have no idea. "None of your business," I say, trying to sound saucy.

The girls hoot all the more. "None of our business! None of our business?" Suddenly Poppy stops hooting and glares at me. "What the hell do you mean none of our business?"

Something fierce and glittering in her eyes frightens me, and I reply honestly. "Nothing. I really wasn't laughing at anything. I mean, I didn't know what I was laughing about." I want to crawl under the floor, into invisibility, into oblivion.

"Leave her alone," Leslie says. "Let's bowl."

Bowling proves the worst disaster yet. My arms seem attached wrong or something, my legs don't move together, and the ball wants to stick to my hand. Instead of gliding gracefully through the air, the ball drops with a thud when I finally manage to release it. It bumps unsteadily toward the gutter, where it settles time and again.

"Another nice one," Poppy says, entering a gigantic zero on the scoreboard with a flourish.

"Too bad," Leslie says. "You'll get it next time." Her kindness feels more like pity to me, and pity tastes almost as sour as sarcasm. Maybe worse.

"The lunch tray can't bowl," Steve says. "What a surprise." *Lunch tray.* This is the first time I've heard that nickname in a while, one I've always hated, maybe because lunches were so lonely before Lori. *Lori. Oh, what have I done?*

Hard to say whose remark is the most painful: to be expected to fail, or to live up to that expectation.

The bowling alley comes alive with lights flashing success when Steve throws strike after strike. Eventually, everyone has tasted success, has thrown at least one strike. Everyone but me.

At first, I'm anxious for my turn, a chance to redeem myself. But I grow to dread it, to anticipate the gutter ball and the giggles of the girls even before it happens. Time after time. But I won't give up, not yet. I utter a silent prayer as I toss my last ball of the game. I won't play again. I had to borrow a quarter from Leslie to have enough for shoes and one game as it is. I try to concentrate on my walk, the release, the aim. I'm hoping for a momentary flash of glory, even if no one cares but me. I want that flash; I *need* that moment.

The ball heads down the center of the lane unsteadily, slowly, but straight for once. Then it veers to the left, only slightly at first, but then more sharply so that just before it makes contact with the pins, it finds, once more, the gutter. My moment has passed.

"Are you going to try again?" Leslie asks, brushing dark straight hair away from the curve of her cheek and hooking it behind a dainty ear.

"No, thanks," I say. "I'll just watch."

The others start a second game while I sit alone, forlornly scratching the mosquito bites on my ankles through my tights, which isn't all that satisfying. They seem to be multiplying. I wonder idly if I've gotten into chiggers instead. Suddenly, I catch a glimpse of movement behind me, and then someone speaks my name.

I jump. The small, wiry man with wild-looking hair sticking out around a red baseball cap grins broadly, as though delighted to see me, and one gold tooth gleams in his smile. "How you doin'?"

THE TICKET

Pee Wee Johnson.

"Fine."

"Spending some of those winnings, are you?"

"Not really."

"Come on, don't tell me it's not making a big difference in your life. A young pretty girl like you."

I'm not pretty, I don't say. So what does he want? "It's not my money, you know."

"No, I guess not. Your pa's not too much into sharing, is he?"

I shrug, not wanting to agree with him but unable to disagree either.

"Well, I'll be seeing you," he says. Then he winks at me. "You can count on that."

"Who was that?" Poppy's voice is thick with distaste.

"Just some friend of my . . . family," I say, embarrassed, but almost beyond embarrassment at this point. Besides, what does it matter really?

"What's he doing here?"

"I don't know. Bowling, I guess." I look around, locating Pee Wee at the snack counter.

"I don't think so," Poppy says. "Kinda gives me the creeps, if you know what I mean."

I do know what she means.

"Say, that's the guy on TV, isn't it?" Steve says. "The one who really bought the ticket."

I nod, and for a few minutes all four of them stare at Pee Wee. I look down at my navy-and-cream bowling shoes, which seem about ten feet long, but out of the corner of my eye, I'm also watching Pee Wee. He glances in my direction for a long moment, then turns his back deliberately on us to address the guy taking orders at the refreshment counter.

"Let's take her home," Steve says, "and see if we can find some action."

"Maybe her dad'll be there," Candy suggests. "I'm about busted."

When I think my humiliation can peak no higher, Poppy

proves me wrong. On the way home, Poppy reaches across Candy to grab my purse. She opens it, searches it, and then turns it upside down to shake out the contents.

"Not a stinkin' dime," she concludes.

"I told you," I say.

"Yep, you told us, but I didn't want to believe it. Is there any point at all in sending you in there to beg?"

I look at Poppy, amazed by her single-mindedness. "No," I say, "there's not."

"It's been real," Steve says, and I catch the hiss from a female voice as I spring from the car. *Bye, Lunch Tray.* Steve screeches the tires as he pulls out of the driveway.

From down the street, I can hear the cars at the Dairy Dip revving their engines, and girlish laughter floating through the night air. But, at this moment, I feel no envy.

I watch Steve's sleek car snake away, glad to see it go.

THE TICKET

CHAPTER THIRTEEN

I JUST WANT to be alone. I don't want to see anybody, or talk to anybody. I throw myself on the bed and try to cry. But the tears do not come.

After a time, I think of Rod Stewart. Rod always cheers me. So I drag myself from the bed, place the needle on my favorite record and listen. He's singing about feeling inferior and combing his hair. I hum along, but it's no use. I simply can't believe Rod ever felt like such a loser as I know I am, always will be. Probably.

Something is wrong. Rod's voice is stuck on a word. "Way . . . way . . . way . . ." The album is scarred. Permanently, irreversibly flawed by a single scratch.

I think of Lori and how I've avoided talking to her, just in case Poppy was trying to call. I groan out loud at my stupidity. I'd been listening to Rod Stewart the first time Poppy called, I recall suddenly, remembering how I jerked the needle on the stereo. Was there a scratching sound then, one I ignored in my haste to get to Poppy?

What a *fool* I've been.

For punishment, I listen to the same note over and over and over until I can't stand it any longer. I don't want to be alone with my thoughts another minute. I think of Gram, then of Mama. Mama has been different lately, almost exuberant, as if she's located some sort of secret delight. I wonder if she's reacting to

THE TICKET

the lottery win, which would be logical but doesn't really strike me as likely.

You never know about people though. Only yesterday, she actually asked me how I was doing, what was on my mind these days. I was so tempted to spill my guts—all my hopes for getting into a popular crowd, for buying some pretty clothes. But something weird in her interest, which was almost feverish, held me back. Her smile and her color were bright, too bright somehow. She practically purred at me.

"Darling girl, we haven't talked in such a long time. I want you to catch me up."

Like we're in the habit of having cozy chats. *Ever*. "On what?"

"Everything."

"Everything?"

"You know, what's going on in your head—your classes, your friends, your life."

Thinking of all the stuff I fairly ached to share, I wavered. In the end, I said, "Oh, you know, just the usual stuff."

"Boys?"

"Boys," I echoed.

"You know, I was your age once. Is there anyone special?"

The image of Rodney Irvine popped immediately to mind. "There's one boy I sort of . . ."

"*Like?*" my mother prompted, her eyes brighter still. "Sort of *like?*"

I nodded, already regretting my admission.

"And does he sort of like you?"

I shook my head. "I don't think so."

"Tell me more, tell me everything," Mama insisted, leaning forward in her chair.

I wished for the millionth time that Mama was more like the busy housewife mothers on TV. That she might ask a question and then get distracted before I answered, like Beaver Cleaver's mom. *That's nice, dear.* Why'd she have to be so honest . . . to really listen when I didn't want her to, and never pretend to be interested just because I needed her to?

The possibility of going out with Poppy and her gang had been so much in the forefront of my mind that I almost blurted out my hopes. But what I said was, "There's nothing to tell," and added quickly, "I made an A on a science test and the highest grade in my English class on my last paper." As I expected, Mama's attention drifted at this news, and I slipped quietly away.

Now I wonder if I did her a disservice. Perhaps, after all, she is someone to talk to, someone less wise than Gram. More human, more selfish, more like me. I should give her a chance.

I locate Mama in the kitchen staring into space. A carton of ice cream rests on the kitchen table in front of her, the ice cream mostly melted and puddling from the carton onto the table. Dripping onto the floor unnoticed.

"Mama?"

My mother turns her head sluggishly toward me. "Yes?"

"Did you know your ice cream is melting?"

"Is it?" She doesn't move.

"If you're finished, I'll put it away for you."

She says nothing, and I wonder if the ice cream is worth saving, but of course we rarely throw anything out in this house. I grab a dish cloth and clean up the mess, wiping the sticky stuff from the bottom of the carton and squeezing it into the freezer compartment of the refrigerator. "I came to talk to you," I say.

My mother looks at me blankly.

I press forward, determined. "You remember yesterday when you wanted me to tell you about my life and everything . . ." My voice trails off as my mother's face remains expressionless. The remnant of hope that she will offer any comfort shrivels inside me, but I plunge ahead anyway. "I just had the most awful experience, and I wanted you—"

I stop, because I can no longer think what it was I wanted her to do or say. There is, after all, *nothing* to be done or said. The hopelessness in Mama's gaze—as though she has seen through life, and there is nothing worth living for—seeps inside me, repelling and frightening me. I think of a song on one of Mama's old record albums, a song I always find depressing: *"Is this all*

THE TICKET

there is?" I am afraid that if I continue with my story, she will reveal some dark truth I cannot bear to hear.

"Never mind," I say. As I leave the room, I glance back, still half hoping she might call after me to prove me wrong—wrong about us both. But Mama sits staring straight ahead, exactly as she was when I entered. I shudder at the contrast in her from one day to the next—from brilliant, fevered interest to dark, distant despair, as if two distinct people live inside her body, like Jekyll and Hyde—a book I both love and hate.

Perhaps what disturbs me most is the part of me that isn't so surprised, the part of me that responds and understands these shifts. I, too, was so hopeful only yesterday, so exhilarated at the opportunity to be part of the in-crowd, to have lots of friends and fit in and laugh and joke. And today I am as dejected as my mother. Gigantic highs and enormous lows.

Is that what I have to look forward to for the rest of my life?

I move in the direction of Gram's space, seeking her calming voice and gentle, predictable touch. Gram leans toward her spit cup as I enter. She's been reading her Bible, chewing on her "toothbrush" as usual, but she removes the stick from her mouth and tucks it away when she catches sight of me. She wipes a small dribble of brown juice from her chin with the back of her hand.

The room is dim and chilly, and I shiver. "Is everything okay?" Gram asks, the permanent line between her brows deepening further.

"Yes," I say. "I mean, no. Everything's awful." The story about Candy and Poppy and Leslie and Steve bursts from me in a flood of words that are nearly incoherent. Even to my own ears.

For a moment, Gram says nothing, even after I've exhausted my breath. Then she says quietly, "Sometimes one of life's hardest lessons is finding out who your real friends are, and who they aren't." She reaches out a hand to pat my head, but I brush it away.

I don't want to hear platitudes. I want, I want . . . I don't know what I want. For Gram to make everything right, I guess, but she can't do that. No one can.

"There's more to it than this, isn't there?" Gram says. "What else is troubling you, child?"

I hesitate. "I went to see Mama."

"I see." A look of sad knowing crosses Gram's face. "And?"

"And . . . what's *wrong* with her, Gram?"

"I don't know. I've never understood your mother's illness."

"I'm afraid," I say. I feel enormously sorry for myself; the tears that would not come earlier in my bedroom spew uncontrollably from my eyes now.

"What are you afraid of?"

I put my head into Gram's lap and sob. She pats my head, waits for me to stop. At last, the tears slow, and I hiccup. "I guess I'm afraid of being like her, of having the illness, too."

For a long moment, Gram doesn't speak, and her silence frightens me way more than anything that has already happened. I realize I've just been waiting for her to reassure me, to tell me that of course I don't have the illness, could *never, ever* have it. But Gram's silence must mean she has the same fear for me, that she sees signs of the sickness in me too.

When Gram finally speaks, her eyes are far away, and her voice refers not to me or even to my mother but to Gram's mother. "When I was a child," she says, "my mother would get sick after every pregnancy. And she had nine children. I didn't know this until my brother was born, and when it happened, I didn't understand. My sister tried to explain it to me, but I still didn't understand. I only knew she needed me more than ever, more than any healthy mother could ever need her daughter. And when all the other girls were gone, I knew I would take care of my mother until the day she died. And I did. It was all I could do. I didn't know how to make the sickness go away, but I couldn't leave her."

"What kind of sickness?" I ask, already knowing the answer.

"It was a kind of sickness of the mind."

"Like Mama's?"

"I guess so. Not exactly though. It was a long time ago, and it was a mystery to me then. It still is."

"So it's an inherited thing. Why didn't you get it?"

THE TICKET

"I don't know that either. None of us did. Maybe it skips a generation."

"Are you saying that if I don't have it, my children probably *will*?"

At the horror in my voice, Gram snaps back to the present. "No, I'm not saying that. I'm just saying I don't understand it. I don't think the doctors do either." She sighs. "The human brain is so complex, and the branch of medicine that deals with mental illness is just a fledgling compared to other parts of the body. Maybe in your lifetime—"

"I can't count on that!" I shriek. "How can I ever hope to get married and raise a family, knowing I could give them some kind of horrible sickness, except for the chance that someday modern medicine might *happen* to stumble on a cure?"

"I don't think you should even worry about it. The chances are that your mother's condition is totally different from my mother's and that it isn't hereditary at all. There's no point in crossing bridges before you get to them, when you may—"

"Then why did you tell me all this? *What were you thinking?*" Suddenly I'm seven years old again, asking Gram about Santa Claus. I hadn't wanted to know. Some mean little boy in my class at school said there was no Santa Claus and, as soon as I got home, I asked Gram, wanting only to be reassured that *of course* there was a Santa Claus. What she said was: "I was hoping you wouldn't find out for a few more years, but I don't want to lie to you."

And with that memory, I hate my grandmother. She has no tact, no sense of how to deal with people. I fling words at Gram, the most damaging I can dredge up. "You're probably right. My mother probably didn't inherit a disease at all. You probably gave it to her by . . . by babying her too much when she was growing up, by never letting her make her own decisions and . . . and whatever. And I may not have any crazy genes at all, but now that you've shared all these stories about your mother with me, I'll never be sure, will I? I'll never be able to have a baby without being afraid. Thanks, Gram. Thanks a lot!"

I run from the room, ignoring the voice of my grandmother trailing after me. Without looking back, I can picture the stricken expression on Gram's face. For one instant, I consider going back and apologizing, telling Gram I didn't mean it. But in the next, all the hurts and hopes and disappointments of the past few days rush in, the painful realization that I will *never* be popular. At least my mother had that. I have inherited only the bad qualities from my mother, none of the good ones. And so I continue to my bedroom, where I throw myself onto the bed and sob.

… THE TICKET …

CHAPTER FOURTEEN

I STARE AT the back of Rodney Irvine's neck, admiring the way his reddish-gold hair springs from tanned skin. As if sensing my gaze, he swings around in his chair to face me. I feel myself blush, and I look quickly away.

"Got your hands on any of that lottery money yet?" he says.

Class hasn't started, and kids are still filtering in. I catch sight of Candy and Poppy entering the room together, laughing and chattering. They pay no attention to me. "No," I admit, looking back at Rodney. He's wearing a crisp white shirt and faded black jeans, and he looks utterly adorable. As usual. "Are you seriously thinking of buying a ticket?"

"Maybe, some day." He shrugs as if the lottery isn't really all that important, and somehow, absurdly, the shrug warms me all over. "Say, would you want to get together to study for that test we're having next Wednesday?" Our eyes meet for a second; his are a bright blue-green, like I imagine the color of the sea to be.

I am speechless. Somehow I never thought of Rodney as someone who studied. Then a wildly absurd thought comes to mind: maybe he likes me. Hope swells and then, almost immediately, shrivels in my chest. No, more likely he is after something. But what? Perhaps . . . maybe . . . he really does just want to study with me. It *could* be as simple as that. "Okay," I say, when I can manage. "When?"

THE TICKET

"I'll call you."

Mr. Ross is rapping a pencil on his desk for attention now, and Rodney swings around to face the front.

My heart hammers against my ribcage so loudly, I worry someone else might hear and comment on it. Foolish, I know, to be excited as if he'd asked me for a date, which he definitely did not. During the next half hour, my emotions soar and plummet like a bird diving for a fish. I'm convinced in one moment that he likes me and in the next that he only wants something from me. I try to picture our study session, but can't do it at all.

Mr. Ross's chalk squeaks on the chalkboard, and I snap back to the present. I hate that noise. I shiver and glance down at my paper, embarrassed to see that I've doodled *Rodney* in several spots on the page, *Rod* in a few others. I mark through the names; glance around furtively to see if anyone has noticed.

"Get out a clean sheet of paper," Mr. Ross announces, and the class lets out a collective groan.

I am silent, but I, too, groan inside. I haven't been paying attention and am bound to mess up royally. Behind me, Rita hisses, "Remember that discount I promised?"

Unfortunately, I cannot forget. As much as I crave new clothes, the image of myself in clothes from her parents' store, like a dressed-up mouse, sends another shudder through my body. I catch a nauseating whiff of strong perfume or cologne.

Rodney likes me, I tell myself. I'm okay; I really am. But, as if from a great distance, I see myself as a tiny, huddled mouse, and Rita as a smug, sharp-clawed cat. "I can get the clothes for you for nothing this time," the cat whispers an octave higher, "for free-ee-ee."

How would you explain a discount to your family, huh, Rita, let alone free clothes? I shift in my seat to make sure Rita can see absolutely nothing.

The hiss persists. "Move over, will you, please? Please!"

There is nothing worth seeing on my paper, even if I *were* inclined to share, which I most definitely am not. Annoyance floods me at the realization that I cannot concentrate with that nagging whisper behind me. I rip the page from my notebook, wad it into a small ball, and whirl around to face Rita.

I smell the powerful perfume clearly now and know for certain Rita is the one exuding the odor. Rita's efforts to camouflage the scent of sweaty desperation have instead heightened it. In spite of her family's affluence and her beautiful clothes, Rita struggles in all of her classes at school. Especially math. Sweat circles darken the lime-colored linen fabric of her expensive blouse, and a few beads of perspiration are visible above her upper lip.

I feel no sympathy. "Would you be quiet so I can concentrate?" I mutter.

"Sure, just move over so I can see, please," Rita whispers back.

"No," I say, more loudly than I intended, my voice seeming to echo through the room. Embarrassed, I glance up just in time to catch Rodney's eye. He has twisted around in his seat and is grinning at me. He gives me a quick "thumbs up" before turning back to his own paper.

THE TICKET

CHAPTER FIFTEEN

On my way to the cafeteria for lunch, I pass a couple of teachers in the hallway and overhear part of their conversation. "It's their age, you know," Miss Williams says. She is one of the younger, more attractive teachers at the school, and dresses stylishly, even provocatively at times. Today she wears a white silk blouse, a tight navy skirt that wrinkles across her shapely hips, very high, high-heeled red pumps, and bright red lipstick. The lipstick is a shade she doesn't normally wear, which makes me wonder if this ensemble is a deliberate tricolor tribute to the upcoming Bicentennial.

"What do you mean?" asks Mrs. Bloomington, who has taught Latin at my school for several decades.

"Raging hormones, that's what," Miss Williams says. "It's no wonder they can't concentrate on history or Latin, or much of anything but the opposite sex."

I move out of earshot at this point, glancing over my shoulder to try to catch the expression on Mrs. Bloomington's face. Mrs. Bloomington nods in apparent agreement, however, and does not appear shocked. I wonder if raging hormones are responsible for my own mood swings, rather than something more ominous. My breasts are starting to grow a little. Not enough to be noticed by anyone else, but enough to make me aware of them. Like buds just beginning to open up inside my new sweater, the one I bought with Lori and her mother. I smile at the image of the buds

THE TICKET

suddenly bursting into full bloom with daisy-like petals poking through my sweater.

The food in the cafeteria actually smells good today, spaghetti with meatballs and garlic bread. I catch sight of Lori sitting alone. My spirits sink at the memory of how mean I've been to her. I ought to feel like scum, which is what I am. Suddenly, I want to talk to someone about Rodney, and Lori is the one I want to tell. But I need to apologize first, and I am rotten at apologizing.

I take my tray to Lori's table. I hope she will act like nothing ever happened, but my voice cracks when I say her name. "Hi, Lori."

"Hi," Lori says without looking up.

"Mind if I sit here?"

"Free country."

"How've you been?"

"Fine."

"You'll never believe what happened to me today." I seat myself across from Lori and lean in so she can hear me without anyone else overhearing.

Lori says nothing, so I continue in a hushed voice. "Do you think Rodney Irvine is cute?"

"Not particularly."

"Why not?"

Lori shrugs. "Not my type."

I know I'm rambling, but I have to persist. "I think he's cute. I guess he *is* my type. Anyway, today, in math class, he asked me if I wanted to study with him." I pause for a second to give Lori a chance to comment. When she does not, I whisper, "I keep wondering if he's after something. Like—like talking to my dad about the lottery or something, but he said to come over to his house—or maybe he just said to get together, I'm not really sure—and so I get to thinking that maybe he likes me or something. And then I think how stupid can you get after what happened last weekend, don't you ever learn a thing? That's what I keep asking myself."

Lori says nothing still. She takes a dainty bite of her ham sandwich. Her nails are polished a silvery lavender color.

I'm wasting my breath, babbling like a fool. Lori hates me,

and I don't blame her. The more I say, the worse I'm making it. But I blunder on anyway. "So you're probably wondering what did happen last weekend. Well, I can't remember if I told you or not—" This is a lie; I know perfectly well that I didn't tell her. "But I was going to go out with Candy and Poppy and that gang, and they were acting like they wanted to be friends, and so we all went to the bowling alley, but I'm a horrible bowler, and I kept throwing them all in the gutter—the balls, that is, not Candy and Poppy and them." I wait for a chuckle or a semblance of a grin, wanting to share the visual of an astonished Poppy bouncing down the lane like the bowling ball. Lori's face is completely blank, so I trudge on. "Of course it turned out they didn't really want to be my friends at all. They just thought I might have come into some money, and when they found out I hadn't, they couldn't take me home fast enough. I felt like such an idiot, you wouldn't believe. Poppy actually went through my purse."

I pause for breath, sure Lori is thinking I'd gotten exactly what I deserved. On top of that, Lori's lack of sympathy is just that much more of what I deserve. The spaghetti is cold now and no longer looks remotely appetizing. I cut the meatballs into smaller sections and slide them about my plate.

"That's awful," Lori says at last, and it takes me a moment to figure out she's talking about Poppy going through my purse.

"Isn't it?" Relief blazes through my body, and only then do I realize how scared I've been, how worried Lori might not forgive me.

"Aren't you hungry?" Lori says.

"I guess not."

"Is it love?" teases Lori, and we laugh.

After I dump my tray, Lori and I leave the cafeteria together. "You really don't think he's cute?" I ask.

"He's not bad," says Lori.

"But, what if he doesn't call? Should I call him?"

"He'll call . . ."

"But what if he doesn't?"

"He will . . ."

THE TICKET

CHAPTER SIXTEEN

I'M ON MY way out of my bedroom, having made up my mind to apologize to Gram, when the phone rings. Since I said such awful things to her, there has been a distance between us. And the distance has kept me from running to her like I usually do with every little thing. I hope the distance between us will melt away as smoothly as with Lori.

I grab the receiver, hoping . . . but it is not Rodney. Lori's voice is cheerful, though, and I am soon laughing and chattering, forgetting my decision to make things up with Gram. "Let's do something," Lori says.

"Like what?"

"We could go to the tennis court. My dad says he'll drive us."

I hesitate for just a second, not wanting to miss a call from Rodney. But that's stupid, a repeat of my mistake with Poppy. "Okay, let's. How soon can you be here?"

We have the tennis courts to ourselves for once. There are only two courts, and on some days we have to wait a while for one to be free. Behind one of the courts is a board with a line drawn at the same height as the net. A player without a partner can practice alone using the board. The net on this court has a hole in it, so we head for the other one, which is farther from the road.

THE TICKET

The day is clear, the sky a brilliant blue. Before we begin the game, we gravitate toward the net and stand there talking for a long time. Lori confides that things at home have not been so good lately.

"But you sounded so cheerful on the phone," I say.

Lori shrugs, her eyes troubled. "I needed to get out of the house. I guess it was sort of an act."

I strive for a light tone. "I didn't know you were such a talented actress."

"I didn't mean to trick you. I just—I guess I just needed you to cheer me up."

I take this in, feeling strong and capable. By the time we start playing, Lori is laughing. And this time, I am pretty sure the laughter is for real.

I'm hitting the ball nice and solid. When I connect with it just so, and it skims over the top of the net, everything feels so right. My spirits lift. The thought flickers across my mind that, only a short time ago, I was so stressed I was ready to sob in Gram's lap. I remember my plan to make up with Gram. Later. I'll make up with Gram later.

I hit my next shot into the net and realize I've lost my concentration. What's wrong with me today? First I couldn't stay focused on my novel, even though it was by Jane Austen, who is just about my favorite writer of all time. All I could think about was why Rodney hadn't called. I kept replaying the scene with him, trying to remember exactly what he said.

Is he going to call the night before the test—or not at all? One thing's for sure. I know he's not agonizing over the call the way I am. Maybe I should just break down and call him.

Life is so complicated. A person's teenage years are supposed to be carefree and filled with fun—the time of your life. That's what my parents seem to think. There is absolutely no way I can ask *them* for advice. They make me feel like such a failure, somebody who can't even get through the charmed part of life with ease. So how in the world will I *ever* survive the rough parts?

"What's wrong?" Lori calls.

"Nothing." There are some things so messed up I can't even share them with Lori. Besides, the day is beautiful, and I don't want to spoil it by being morbid. Scooping the ball up between my foot and racket, I bounce it once with the racket to catch it tidily, a new trick I've been practicing. I back paddle to the service line. "I'm going to try a serve. Are you ready?"

Lori nods, and I toss the ball high into the air. I catch a glimpse out of the corner of my eye of someone walking onto the court next to me. I sense the person is watching me serve, which makes me suddenly self-conscious. My serve lands inside the correct square, but instead of skimming the net, the ball soars high into the air and then drops abruptly into the box.

I glance at the man to see if he is snickering. But he nods approvingly. "Keep practicing," he says. "The serve is the hardest part of the game when you're starting out."

It is the same man who complimented me before when we were here. He turns toward the backboard and hits a ball against it. He's mostly bald, with just a dark ring running around the back of his head; the late afternoon sunlight glistens off the top of what's left of his hair. I remember the other man, also middle-aged with a slight paunch over his belt, who was with him the first time I saw him here. Mr. Compliments has a gut, too. He's bigger all over than the other guy, especially around the middle, like he drinks beer every night or something.

I wonder if he's waiting on his partner now. I turn my attention back to my serve, and work at it hard for a while. "Whew!" I say finally. "Let's take a break. I need some water." I wipe my brow.

"You're getting better," Lori says, while I drink thirstily.

Pleased she thinks so, I pass the thermos to Lori. "You want to serve some?"

"I don't know. You know what's going to happen. We'll spend all our time chasing the balls."

"You know what we need? A bunch of balls—"

"Like he has?" With a slight tilt of her head, Lori indicates the man, who is still alone, hitting against the backboard. He'd brought a large bucket of balls, many of which are dotted about

THE TICKET

the court and the grass around its edges.

"Yeah, like that," I agree. "But balls cost money. A bucket of balls that size must cost . . ." I hesitate, doing some rapid mathematics in my head, ". . . way more than I can afford. Anyway, I don't mind chasing balls. Not so much."

Lori, true to her word, hits the balls wildly, and the second one nearly reaches the backboard on the next court. "Sorry," I mumble to the man, crossing over to retrieve the ball.

"No problem." He smiles at me, but does not meet my eyes. "You're looking good."

"I'm getting better anyway," I say.

"No, I didn't mean your game. I meant you."

"*Me*?"

He looks me up and down in a way that makes me blush. "You've got a head start on a fine womanly figure."

No one has ever said such a thing to me before. Certainly not a man. I feel curiously pleased, but also a little uneasy. My face tingles hotly. Before I can think how to respond, he is talking again, while his eyes appraise me openly.

"You just need a little more up here." He gestures to my chest. "Not a lot, you understand, but a little more. How old are you, fifteen—sixteen?"

"Fourteen."

"Even better. More time—to develop, you know."

I stare at the man, wide-eyed, still speechless, though a retort comes to mind. "And you might grow up to be pretty good looking yourself," I could say, "when you grow some hair and lose some of that baby fat."

Of course, I'd never say such a thing out loud, but the thought makes me smile, and I know that later I'll tell Lori and we'll have a good laugh. I am downright pleased with myself for coming up with a rejoinder for once in my life, even if I don't have the nerve to say it. Maybe there's hope for me after all.

"Look!" Lori calls out.

"Where?"

"Behind you. Do you know that man?"

At first, I imagine Lori to be referring to the man on the next court. I whirl around. Behind the fence, resting against his bike, lurks Pee Wee Johnson. Pee Wee is wearing long pants and a dingy muscle shirt that was probably white once, and there is no racket in the basket of his bike. Seeing me turn in his direction, Pee Wee lifts a tattooed arm. He holds a tennis ball. "This yours?"

"I don't think so." I hide my dismay at seeing him here. "We've got all our balls, don't we?" I call to Lori.

"One, two, three." Lori points them out. "Yep."

"It must be his." I point to the man on the next court.

"Oh, well, in that case . . ." Pee Wee shrugs, dropping the ball on the ground.

Lori and I continue our game, but my mood is completely ruined. My skin crawls. I look over my shoulder to see if Pee Wee is still there. I don't see him, and not knowing where he is makes me even less comfortable somehow. "You ready to go?" I ask Lori.

"We'll have to go somewhere to call. Dad won't be here for another half hour or so. You sure you want to leave?"

"Yeah, there's something I want to talk to you about." I can't remember if I told Lori about seeing Pee Wee at the bowling alley or not, but I'm going to tell her now. I keep my eyes focused on where we're going, not looking back at the man on the next court as we leave. I feel his eyes following me, though, and I imagine another pair of eyes on me as well. A shiver runs through me. I walk briskly so that Lori has to struggle to keep up.

We head toward the corner gas station.

"What's the big rush?" Lori gasps. Her cheeks are bright pink, and her hair forms damp curls around her face. She looks faintly annoyed.

"I'll tell you when we get there," I say.

THE TICKET

CHAPTER SEVENTEEN

On Saturday, Lori and I spend the entire day together. We have a great time all morning, and it just about takes my mind off Rodney and why he hasn't called yet. But then, somehow, we end up in Gram's room with Lori spilling her guts.

"He's punched a hole in one of the doors before," Lori tells Gram. Lori's wearing a brand new pair of green-and-tan plaid, polyester pants and a turtleneck sweater with soft-green-and-gold flecks. Though it hasn't bothered me until now, suddenly it strikes me as supremely unfair that her mom is banned from just about every store in town and she still winds up with new clothes all the time, while my dad wins the lottery and I don't even get one new outfit out of it.

"Tray knows about that," Loris is saying. "But this time he hit the glass in the patio door, and pieces of glass went everywhere. His hand was dripping blood like crazy. He had to go to the emergency room and get it stitched up. It was so awful!"

A large teardrop stands in one of Gram's pale blue eyes. "I'm so sorry you had to experience that," she says.

I understand enough to be ashamed of the pang of jealousy that shoots through me at the way Gram and Lori have hit it off. I'm not exactly sure which of the two I'm actually jealous of, both I guess. I like being strong for Lori, being her confidante, and now here she is, pouring out her heart to Gram. *My* Gram.

THE TICKET

I never got around to apologizing to Gram for the hateful things I said that day. I don't know why apologies have to be so danged tough. But since Gram seems ready to go on as if I'd never said anything wrong, that's just fine with me.

Besides, Gram knows how I feel about her, doesn't she? I'll find the right words one of these days.

"The trouble with parenting," Gram says, "is that most of us manage to muddle through it before we've had the time—or taken the time—to think about how our actions affect our children. We get so caught up in the moment, we just don't think. I'm sure that's what's happening at your house."

Lori lays her head in Gram's lap, a spot usually reserved for mine, and sobs. When she lifts her head, her eyes are wet with tears, but bright. Hopeful. She turns to where I stand off to one side, kicking the toe of my sneaker into the rug. "Tell Gram about your contest," Lori says.

I don't know whether to be annoyed or proud that Lori has started referring to Gram as *Gram*. "There's nothing to tell," I say. "It was a stupid idea."

"*What?*" Gram says. "What was a stupid idea?"

Lori's and Gram's eyes are on me now, and I shrug. "Nothing really."

"Get the magazine and show her," Lori urges. "There's this contest, see . . ."

Why not? Pulse racing, I head in the direction of my room without waiting to hear the rest of Lori's sentence.

When I return with the magazine and hold it out to Gram, it falls open to the page describing the fashion design competition. Gram places her reading glasses on her nose and reads slowly. Impatiently, I shift from one leg to the other, swinging an imaginary tennis racket and resisting the temptation to peer over Gram's shoulder. I know the rules of the contest by heart anyway.

"So what do you think?" I say when Gram finally finishes and looks up.

"You should go for it, of course."

"That's what I told her," Lori chimes in.

"But I'm so... so... *inexperienced*. What if the other entries are all so much better that mine is a joke by comparison?"

"Maybe yours will be fresh and original by comparison," Gram says. "What do you have to lose?"

"That's exactly what I said!" Lori says, and I shoot her a look.

I'm not sure what I have to lose exactly, but I don't want to set myself up for almost certain failure either. If I am going to enter the competition, I want my design to be good. Really, really good. So far I haven't come up with a single good thing.

"Have you been working on a design already?" Gram asks, as if reading my mind.

I shrug.

"May I see them?"

"I tore them all up. They weren't any good—"

"They were too," Lori interrupts. "I saw some of them, and I thought they were pretty awesome."

"What about some of your old designs? Couldn't you revamp one of those?" Gram suggests.

I shake my head. "I don't think so." I've been operating on the assumption that I need to create something new. I think back now to the stack of drawings in my dresser drawer. There is one that just might...

With a jolt, I see a variation of the style in my head. Without a word of explanation—fearful the image might vanish as quickly as it appeared—I dash to my room to grab a pad and pencil. I work rapidly, frenetically, until I have the design on paper. Then I suck in a deep breath and copy the image more slowly, carefully this time, with a few alterations, onto another page.

Pleased with the result, I stare at the page, afraid what I think is good in this moment will sour by the next. Barely breathing, I carry the page, as gently as if it were a breakable heirloom, to Gram's room to show Gram and Lori.

"I love it!" Lori says at once.

Gram looks at the drawing for a long time, while my heart thumps furiously in my chest. Gram is going to be honest. I can feel it, and I'm afraid it isn't good. Would she choose this moment

THE TICKET

to tell me the ugly truth?

"I think you have something here," Gram says, and Lori squeals with delight. "I think you should enter this in the contest."

The drawing is of a fairly simple denim dress, designed with narrow straps, a deep V-neckline, and a flared skirt striking well above the knee. A hint of a lace ruffle edges the V of the neckline, and a deeper expanse of ruffled slip shows below the hemline. I see the dress in a dusky blue, the slip a snowy white. The bodice has simple vertical stitching down the center from the point of the V to the waist and, horizontally, straight across beneath the bust. Over the bodice, I have drawn a sweet blouse with tiny sleeves, puffed just the least bit and clinging loosely to the upper arm, a casual double collar, and no visible buttons. The overlayer hangs open to reveal the denim bodice, and a leather belt is looped over the blouse (red, maybe, to complete the bicentennial tricolor—am I becoming obsessed with this tricolor thing?), the buckle dangling slightly to accentuate the wearer's tiny waistline. The fabric of the blouse is not ruffled, but an opaque filmy fabric, defined in my drawing by a series of fine lines. The collar, in contrast, is smooth.

"Do you think she might need some accessories?" Gram says. "Or at least some shoes?"

I take the drawing from my grandmother, add a leather band to the model's wrist to match the belt and a pair of thick-soled canvas sandals with cork soles and tasseled ties around the ankles.

"Now she's perfect." Lori claps her hands.

"I don't know." I'm pleased with their reaction but still uncertain. Maybe the tassels aren't right. "I just don't know. Maybe I should try for something more exotic. Maybe it's too simple."

"That's its charm," Gram says.

I think so too, but I'm afraid of being wrong. When I first saw the contest in this magazine—and it just happened to be on a day when I had enough money to pay for it—it struck me as a sort of sign. Now I'm more skeptical. My family has already been lucky once this year with the lottery win. What are the odds that luck would strike twice in the same year?

The winner of the contest gets to fly to New York to meet with real fashion experts from the magazine staff, plus a chance to present her work, or his, in a special edition. It's way too much to dream. If I let myself hope again, I'll just be setting myself up for more disappointment. Like with Poppy. So I say once more, "I don't know."

"You've got to try," Lori says. "How could you forgive yourself if you didn't even try?"

I look from my friend to my grandmother, whose faded blue-gray eyes are sort of twinkling their agreement. "All right," I say at last. "I'll give it a try."

Lori squeals again, and she and I whirl around a few times in a gleeful dance. "I just know you're going to win!" Lori says, and I long with all my being for her to be right.

For the next hour, Lori watches while I work, trying different variations of the design, experimenting with the use of colored pencils and crayons, as well as black & white. I finally settle on one of the earlier versions, using a combination of pencil shading and colored pencils. I like the red, white, and blue theme for the bicentennial, but I worry that everyone's doing that. My heart thuds as I seal it inside the envelope and I think that maybe I *should* have gone with a black and white draft. I almost rip into the envelope to reconsider, but Lori stops me.

Gram gives me a few postage stamps so we won't have to find a ride to the post office, and Lori and I head to the mailbox.

A man on a bike rounds the corner headed in our direction just as we get to the mailbox. When he is near enough to be heard, he says, "Is your dad home?"

Pee Wee Johnson. "No." I shake my head and exchange a meaningful glance with Lori. "He isn't."

"So what are you handling with such care?"

"It's nothing important."

"Tray's entering a contest!" Lori bursts out. "And if she wins, she'll get to go to New York and meet all sorts of famous fashion designers." I redden, wondering what sort of insanity has possessed my friend.

"Is that right?" Pee Wee brakes his bike and stands, one foot on the pedal and one on the ground. He's close. Too close for my comfort. "*Is that right?*" he repeats. "Wouldn't that be something—two wins in one year?"

Strange, hearing my own thought uttered aloud. I mutter, "Not much chance of that, I'm afraid."

"You sure your dad's not home?"

"I'm sure." Annoyed, I close the mailbox lid and turn to go.

Lori follows me, and Pee Wee calls after us. "Tell your dad I was here, won't you? Tell him he'd better be doing the right thing."

I glance over my shoulder just in time to catch a glimpse of Pee Wee shaking his fist in the direction of the house as he wheels off on his bike.

CHAPTER EIGHTEEN

Lori and I are back in the house, and I'm shaky but exhilarated at surrendering my hopes and dreams to the care of the mailman. When the doorbell rings, I think at first that Pee Wee has returned. "I told you he wasn't here," I'm prepared to say.

This rebuff gives way to a wordless stare when a slender man, much younger than Pee Wee, with neatly styled blond hair, a hint of blonde stubble on his chin, and bright blue eyes smiles at me. "Is your father home?"

"Not yet." I sigh. "He should be here soon."

"Is it okay if I wait?"

I hesitate, thinking of all the warnings I've heard over the years about talking to strangers. But this man doesn't look threatening. And, although I know from reading tons of mysteries that you can't always judge a person's motives by his appearance, I'm pretty sure my instinct is right this time. I show him into the den, curious about his business, while Lori looks on. Somehow, he doesn't strike me as the sort of person to be begging for charity, but why else would he be here?

"He is *so cute!*" Lori says as soon as we're out of earshot.

"He is, isn't he?"

A few minutes later, the doorbell rings again. This time it's is a tired-faced woman about Mama's age, also looking for Dad. I escort her into the den too.

THE TICKET

"You know why they're here, don't you?" I ask Lori.

Lori shakes her head.

"You can be sure it has something to do with the lottery. It's because they aired that stupid thing on TV with the check and all."

"Oh, so that's why you look so perturbed." I love it that Lori, like me, often comes out with these words you wouldn't normally hear from the mouth of kids our age. "Aren't you getting tired of it?"

"I've got an idea," I say. "Why don't we put up a sign?"

We scramble for materials and, giggling all the while, tape our notice on the front door.

HE'S NOT HERE. GO AWAY PLEASE.

When Dad does finally get home, Lori and I meet him between his car and the door. I figure since I let them in, I should be the one to warn him.

"Did it help?" he asks, indicating the sign with a dry chuckle.

"Not really. Maybe. There are three people waiting in the den to talk to you, but only one of them came after we put up the sign."

"They've been bugging me all day at the office, too." He sighs and loosens his gray and navy striped tie. "The reporters, and the brokers who want to *help* me invest the money, and the women with diseased children or dying parents. The list just keeps getting longer."

"You're keeping a list?" I'm impressed that he might actually be trying to prioritize the demands.

"No, it was just a figure of speech." He looks tired, the bags under his eyes and the lines in his face deeper than usual.

"Do you sometimes wish you hadn't won it, Dad?"

"No, no, I don't wish that."

"But it seems like such a hassle. I can't see that it's making anything better."

Dad catches his upper lip between his teeth. "No, it doesn't, does it? But that's just because I haven't sorted it all out yet."

I shrug. "I guess you should go see what those people want."

He asks me to tell them he'll be there shortly, and he heads to the bathroom. When he comes out, Lori and I listen in the hallway. The cute guy speaks first. "I want you to help me to pick my number for the next one."

"The next one?" Dad echoes.

I know what he means. I suspect Dad does too. "The lo-lottery," he says, stammering a little in his fevered excitement. "I have to win this one, you see. And so I thought the way—the best way—the best chance would be if you'd be so kind, you could help me out so's some of your luck might rub off on me. You see?"

"I didn't pick that number myself," Dad says. "I am not really what you'd call a lucky person."

The man sounds disbelieving. "You won't even try?"

I feel bad for the man, and for Dad. "Let's get out of here," I say to Lori.

"Okay. Where to?"

"Outside, I guess. We can go around back." I grab my tennis racket and a couple of balls. Lately I've gotten really good at juggling them on the racket. I flip it back and forth so that I use different sides on alternate hits.

"Aren't we ever going back to the courts?" Lori asks once we're outside.

I snag the tennis ball in the air with my hand and take a broad swing. "I doubt if Dad wants to be bothered right now."

"Maybe he'd be glad of an excuse to get away," Lori counters.

"Hmm," I say, thinking this is actually not a bad idea. "Maybe he would."

"I can get my dad to pick us up after."

A new arrival, a tall, stooped man with a receding hairline, finds us in the backyard before we can escape. "We were just leaving," I tell him, thinking I should breeze past without slowing down.

The tall man looks as if he expected as much, and I hesitate in the face of his defeated stance. "What did you—uh—need?"

"I just wanted to talk to your dad for a minute."

"What about?" Although I know, *how I know*, Dad's been bombarded with sad stories, I simply can't help feeling

THE TICKET

sympathetic to this man's tale of being laid off from work, on top of medical bills for a daughter with leukemia and fees for a special school for a mentally disabled son.

"I'll tell my dad," I say, taking a carefully folded piece of paper from him. A faint glimmer of hope brightens the man's eyes, and I notice he's walking a little straighter when he leaves. "You might check back in a day or two," I call after him.

As it turns out, Lori is right about Dad being glad of an excuse to escape. I tell him about the tall stooped man's troubles on our way to the tennis court. "Don't you just wish you could help them all?" I ask.

Dad shoots me a curious look, glances away and then back, sort of like a squirrel in the middle of the road trying to decide which way to run. "I can't say that I do," he says slowly. "But maybe I should. Could be you've got something there."

There's no sign of the fat man or Pee Wee when we arrive. For a time, we play hard. Lori is not hitting well today, but my shots are better than ever—maybe the last few days away from the courts have actually *helped* my game. As always, Lori is a good sport and laughs at her own wild shots. For a second, I wish I had someone better to play with, but I shrug off that thought as disloyal, a road I've already been down once—and that's once too often.

"I've got to go to the bathroom," Lori says after a time. "Want to come?"

The nearest restroom is at the gas station on the corner and I don't need to go yet. "No, I'll just stay and practice against the backboard till you get back."

While I'm waiting, the sky darkens. I glance up, hoping the rain will hold off until we finish playing. I hit a ball too hard; it soars over the board and behind the fence. I mutter under my breath at my lack of control and go to retrieve the ball. When I return, the fat man is there.

"How ya doing today?" he asks with a broad smile. His teeth are very straight, almost too perfect. Probably dentures.

"I'm fine."

"What you need is a basket of balls. Like I have." He indicates his own basket. "So you won't have to spend all your time chasing after them."

I glance longingly at the full basket.

"Look, I've got another basket full in my car. I'm more than happy to give it to you."

"Oh, no, I couldn't."

"Really. I was going to throw them away. They're getting kind of flat, you know, but they're better than nothing." He motions me to follow as he moves off in the direction of his car. He pauses for me to catch up, but I hesitate. "My car is just over here. Follow me and I'll get you those balls."

I take a step or two, then waver. He motions again. "Come on. You won't believe what a difference it'll make in your game."

Seduced by the dual vision of a full bucket of balls and an improved game, I follow the man to a two-door dirt-colored Chevrolet. "I know they're here somewhere," he says, opening the door on the driver's side. "Look in the back floorboard, and I'll check the trunk."

A voice inside me that's wiser than I am says there's something not quite right here. I vacillate, wanting to run and find Lori but unsure, not wanting to be rude, and still lusting for the balls. Probably, almost certainly, the man is just trying to be nice, after all, and I'm being silly and paranoid. Too many "don't talk to strangers" lectures from Dad and Gram have gotten into my head and left me confused about my own judgment.

As soon as I lean in, I know I've made the wrong choice. Before I can pull back, he shoves me, hard, and slides in beside me.

"What—what are you doing?" I gasp. I scoot away from him toward the passenger's side, burning the backs of my legs on the fabric of the seat. He squeezes against me so tightly I cannot turn in the seat.

This isn't happening, I think. I reach for the passenger door handle, jerk it, but the door does not open. Panic rises in my chest.

"I'll get you those balls. I just want to show you something first," he says. I can smell his breath now, a mixture of spaghetti sauce and beer. There's also the hint of Dentyne, like he tried to hide a giant clove of garlic with a tiny stick of red gum. "Then I'll get the balls out of the trunk." I'm barely breathing, not wanting to inhale his breath, terrified that he might put his mouth on mine.

But what happens is worse, *so much worse.*

He unzips his pants and reaches in like he's digging for ice cream at the bottom of a dipping carton. I recoil in surprise and horror. I know, though I've never seen one up close, that what he pulls out is something I shouldn't be seeing. My eyes widen. Something acidy rises in my throat. I think to scream, but nothing comes out. I turn wildly toward the door, pull at the handle again, but he pins me more tightly than ever so I cannot reach the lock.

"Wouldn't you like to touch it?" he says, his tone coaxing, his breath ragged. "Just one little touch?"

I shake my head so violently I hear the bones in my neck crack. I press myself against the door, repelled and frightened, and strangely fascinated.

"I won't make you if you don't want to," the man purrs. Again his breath catches. "But I just wanted you to see what you do to me."

"I'd like to get out please." My voice comes out as a mouse-like squeak.

"Not just yet." The man grabs his thing and begins to jerk it up and down. I twist my head away to avoid both the sight and the smell before me. I'm staring at the kudzu taking over the space behind the tennis court when a face appears at the car window next to me. Pee Wee. For a second, I think it's a conspiracy, the two of them against me. "Damn," the fat man mutters.

I see immediately that Pee Wee's face is livid with rage. He moves to the driver's side and bangs on the window. "What the hell's going on?"

Thank goodness, Pee Wee's anger is directed at the fat man. I find my voice and scream. "*Help me!*"

Pee Wee yanks at the driver-side door and, to my relief, it swings open. "I didn't hurt her," the man says with his hands up and that snake-like thing now lying limp between his legs. Pee Wee slams his fist into the man's face. I tug at my door again, which still won't open. Forcing myself to think calmly, I am able to locate the lock and open the door.

I tumble out onto the ground, shuffle my feet until I am standing again on legs that tremble badly. I run past the front of the car, look over my shoulder. Pee Wee's fists are flailing at the man's face. I look the other way, down the street, and see Lori approaching the courts, unaware that anything has happened in her absence.

"If you ever so much as show your face around here again," Pee Wee is shouting, "you'll be sorry, and that's a promise."

Glancing at the sky, I see the dark cloud has passed over. It isn't going to rain after all. The sinking sun glows sweetly in the late afternoon sky, the colors more brilliant than any in my box of colored pencils and crayons, mystical blends of lavenders and golds, with silver-rimmed swirls of deep aqua. So much beauty amidst such ugliness.

A cool breeze caresses my cheek. I glance at my wristwatch, thinking surely an hour has gone by. But no—*how little time has passed.*

"Hey, Tray!" Lori hollers.

I take off running then, to carry myself to Lori as fast as I can. I'm shaking when I reach her. I throw myself into her arms and sob out as much of the story as I can manage.

We turn and look back at the Chevrolet, where Pee Wee still leans in, still shakes his fist, still shouts. The fat man manages to start his car. It careens in reverse, then shoots forward. The tires screech as he drives off, throwing Pee Wee off balance. The little man collects himself and turns toward me and Lori.

"Are you okay?" he asks, just loud enough for me to hear. His face is red, and he too sounds shaken.

"I'm fine," I say, but my voice is unsteady.

Pee Wee walks toward us, brushing imaginary dirt from his hands. I totally get that. I feel filthy too. "I'm calling the police," he says, and I nod. "They'll probably want to talk to you to verify things."

I'm trembling so badly now my teeth rattle, but I shake my head. "Please don't. If you do, I'll never be allowed to come here again." Pee Wee's expression registers just enough indecision to encourage me to press my point. "Besides, I think he's too scared to come back. Even if he does, I don't think he'll bother me again."

"But what if he bothers someone else?" Pee Wee says. "Don't we have a responsibility to prevent that?" This sounds reasonable, but I feel older than Pee Wee about now. Maybe it's because I've read more books. "Even if you do call the police, nothing will happen to him—because he didn't really *do* anything. The most that could happen is that they would try to scare him, and you've already done that."

Pee Wee looks doubtful. "Are you sure you're okay?" he says, and all I can think is how remarkably different he seems to me right now than all the times I've seen him in the past. Protective. Almost *fatherly*. "Do you want me to walk you home or find a taxi or something?"

I hesitate for a second, and Lori says, "No, thanks. My dad should be here any minute."

"I'll just hang around until your father gets here, to make sure *he* don't come back."

"Thanks," I say, and I mean it.

Lori squeezes my hand so hard it hurts. We sit together on the concrete, silent for a time, breathing heavily still. I long to do something to ease the tension. "Let's hit a few more balls," I say after a few minutes, "while we wait."

Lori raises her eyebrows in surprise, then shrugs her assent. My shots are shaky at first but, after a few hits, I find I can control them by gripping the racket more tightly than usual and hitting the balls harder. I hit them so hard, in fact, one narrowly misses Lori's head, zooming past her ear with unprecedented speed.

"Hey, watch out," Lori calls.

"Sorry." After that, I direct my shots away from my friend. For several minutes, I take my anger and confusion out on the ball. Some of my shots soar over the fence and out into the grass, but a few of them skim the net and land just inside the back line with satisfying intensity, sweetly slicing through the air . . . the exact way I would like to slice through the fat man's arrogance.

CHAPTER NINETEEN

When I tell Gram what happened, her reaction is more annoying than helpful.

"We have to tell your dad."

"*No.*" I'm emphatic.

"Why not?"

"If we tell him, I'll never be allowed to play tennis again. I knew I shouldn't have told you either!"

"But are you willing to go back there," Gram says, "and risk seeing him again?"

"Yes." I can hear the defiance in my voice, so I try to lessen it a little. "I think I am. And, besides, I really don't think he'll come back. Not after what Pee Wee said to him."

"I don't know if you should. If I let you go and something happens—something bad—I could never forgive myself."

"Is that all you worry about—being able to forgive yourself?"

"No, of course not," she says. "I'm worried about you."

"But you weren't there. When Pee Wee showed up and did what he did, that man was scared speechless. Even though he's so much bigger than Pee Wee, there was something about Pee Wee—something fierce."

"But Pee Wee might not be there the next time," Gram points out.

"Pee Wee scared him off for good. I'm sure of that."

––––––––––––––– THE TICKET –––––––––––––––

"Then why are you shaking?" Gram strokes my hair.

"Oh, Gram." I throw myself across Gram's lap. "It's just—I've always known there are people like him in the world. But I never thought I'd—you know—run into one of them myself."

When I shut my eyes at night, I see the fat man, his face, his belly, his hairy private parts. Listening to the familiar sounds of crickets outside and teenagers squealing tires or revving their motors, I shudder at the images that haunt me. I search for happy things to take their place, like the lightning bugs that brush up against the windows when it's dark outside. Sometimes when I'm at school, I can be right in the middle of English class, listening to a really nice poem, and suddenly something triggers the memory. I squeeze my eyes shut, willing it away. *I will not think of it, I will not dwell on it, I won't, I won't, not ever.*

Thank heaven Pee Wee showed up when he did. Who'd have ever in a million years guessed I'd be thinking *that*?

Sometimes, I mull over my conversation with Gram, wondering if I should, after all, confide in Dad. Every time, though, I decide against it—I mean, what good could possibly come of it? Besides which, if word of what happened spread around school, I would be positively *mortified*.

I watch for the mail every single day, no matter how hard I try not to. When I submitted my entry, the deadline was so close I figure notification could come any moment. The mailman, Mr. Green, delivers the mail around the time I get home from school, sometimes earlier, sometimes later. As soon as I come home, I rush to see if it's arrived.

Usually, if the mail has run, Gram's already picked it up and left it on the table in the foyer. When there's no mail lying around, I watch furtively for the mailman's car. Maybe my entry was so poor, they won't even bother to notify me I didn't win because it's *so obvious*.

When I've just about given up, the envelope comes.

Mr. Green is running late. Even though I'm no longer expecting the arrival, I'm still watching. I try to look nonchalant as I reach for the stack, but of course Mr. Green sees right through me.

"Anything today?" he says while I'm flipping through the variously sized envelopes.

When I read the return address of one slim blue envelope, I freeze for a moment, visions of traveling to New York City dancing like sugarplums in my head. Coming back to Kentucky earth, I nod to Mr. Green, and he gives me a thumbs-up. I carry the envelope, heart pumping furiously, to my bedroom and close the door quietly. For a moment, I just hold the envelope, afraid to read the contents, and even more afraid for anyone else to be watching when I do.

My fingers tremble as I rip into the thin blue envelope. I stare at the ragged edges, trying to prepare myself. And then I am clutching the letter, my fingers thick and awkward. *Congratulations*, I read, and hope explodes in my chest.

I read on. My entry has been awarded honorable mention, along with several others. Honorable mention, I mutter to myself as my heart slows its frenetic pace. *Honorable. Honor.* What does that mean, really, except that *I lost*? My head spins, and I grasp the edge of my desk to steady my shaking legs. How can there be honor in losing, I wonder. Or, for that matter, in winning?

I think of Dad, of his dilemma about how to spend the lottery money and whether to share it with Pee Wee. My head fills with questions, but no answers. Should he spend it all on our family— *we do need it, goodness knows* . . . should he help Gram move out, or should he help some of those miserable souls who plead their cases daily? Is it possible that if I'd won, I would have been lured by the glamor of the people I'd meet, come home to scorn the people who really love me? People like Gram and Lori. I remember the fiasco with Poppy and Candy and try to feel better.

And yet, I wanted it *so* much. I throw myself across the bed and beat my fists into my pillow. I sob out my disappointment, no longer caring who hears. I don't really believe winning would have corrupted me, and telling myself it is just sour grapes, the punchline of one of Gram's stories: "Them grapes was probably sour anyway." I cry and cry until I'm nearly cried out.

Eventually, I become aware of someone knocking at the door,

THE TICKET

almost in time to the rhythm of my hiccupy breath. I rub my eyes with a fist and rise slowly, as if in a trance. When I open the door, there's Dad, his face strained with anxiety.

"What's wrong?"

I honestly don't know where to begin, too overcome by everything that's wrong. All the hope, and all the disappointment: for the clothes I'll never own, for the popularity that will always elude me, for the honorable girl I will never become. I fling myself into my father's arms and weep against his shoulder. The last time I did this, my head only reached his chest. I am getting as tall as a giraffe, and this thought makes me cry harder.

"There, there." Dad pats me awkwardly. "Whatever it is, you can tell me."

I lift my head and meet his troubled green gaze. Can I tell him? *Should* I tell him?

The face of the fat man, his voice telling me he wants to show me something, the mental images I want to erase: it's all there, just waiting for room to surface.

Suddenly it occurs to me that this is a once-in-a-lifetime opportunity to connect with this man who, despite his foibles, loves me. I open my mouth, and the words tumble out. Dad drops onto the edge of my bed while I talk, while I pace around the word. In some part of my brain, I know I'm telling him everything, but the one thing I should. I make up for the omission with a surplus of details; the stories jumbled. Rita Davis's party, the bowling nightmare with Candy and Poppy, the competition I wanted so badly to win. Finally, I show him the honorable mention letter, and he reads it out loud. I perch on the bed beside him, peering over his shoulder. There is to be a picture of my drawing, along with all the other honorable mentions, in an upcoming issue.

"That's terrific!" he says, looking perplexed at my disappointment.

Hiccupping back more tears, I explain what I'd been hoping for, what the winner would receive. When at last, out of breath, I pause and draw a shaky breath, I find myself oddly calm. Dad and I are sitting side by side now, on the edge of my bed, staring straight out, not at each other. My moment of what had seemed an epiphany has vaporized now, along with the dream of New York City, of meeting people who could open doors for me, who might help me to find my path in life. All gone.

I wait for Dad to say something. To make it better somehow. (*How*? Do I really think he's going to fly me to NYC with the lottery money and barge our way into fashion headquarters?)

Dad looks at a loss. His shoulders slump, so I square mine. "How was *your* day, Dad?" I ask.

He laughs, an odd laugh, sort of a cross between a snort and a whinny. I peer into his eyes, trying to read this man who lives in the same house and yet in a different world from me. "What's funny?" I say.

"I'm not laughing at you. I'm relieved, I guess, that you're cried out." He pauses. "Are you cried out?"

"I think so."

"I've never been good with female tears. Makes me feel helpless or something. That's not why I'm laughing though, not exactly . . . I guess I'm laughing at my day."

"Was it . . ."

"Awful? Yep, it was pretty awful."

"What happened?"

"People just kept calling and calling, and coming to the office. Like a plot to drive your old man stark-raving mad."

I wait for him to go on. When I'm starting to think he isn't going to, he continues. "What happened today was I decided I wouldn't answer. I would just let it ring. And ring it did. It rang and it rang and it rang. Until we were all going nuts."

"What did you do?"

"I jerked the phone right out of the wall."

I giggle. "How did that go over?"

Dad stares at me for a second, and then he, too, bursts into laughter. This time it's a good sort of laughter that starts in the belly and works its way up until your eyes stream. I try to remember the last time my father and I laughed together like this and can't. "They looked sort of stunned. It was pretty funny, but nobody laughed—until now."

"I still wish we could help them all."

"Well, we can't." His voice goes flat, and he rises to leave. Our moment of mirth is all but forgotten. "There's not that much money. It's not going to go very far, once we start letting it go—"

"What about Pee Wee? Are we at least going to share some with him?"

Dad looks annoyed. "Your mother's right about him. He's just a splinter in my foot."

"I don't think he's so bad."

"Why would you say that?" He's at the door now, but he looks back at me, one eyebrow lifted in surprise.

"Because." I shrug. "Just because." Why does it keep haunting me, this ugly thing I want so badly to eradicate? I don't want a big stink made about the incident and I don't want Dad to prevent me from playing tennis. If I tell, the tennis courts will be off-limits for sure, and where else can I play? I make a show of smoothing my bed covers, fluffing my pillows, looking anywhere but into Dad's curious eyes.

"Is there something you're not telling me?"

I hesitate just an instant, then shake my head. I've shared enough for one day.

CHAPTER TWENTY

When I come home from school, I'm surprised to find Mama and Pee Wee standing together in the back yard. A neighbor has been burning trash or leaves or something. They're actually standing in the neighbor's yard, staring at the fire as if it has hypnotic powers over them.

The neighbor, watching from his patio, glances in my direction, and I lift a hand to wave. I shrug, as if to say, grownups can be pretty weird sometimes, which is what I'm thinking. Of course, he's a grownup himself. I wander out to the fire to say hello to Mama and Pee Wee.

"I love to watch things burn," Pee Wee says. "Don't you?"

"Not especially," I start to say. But then I realize he isn't talking to me. I glance down at the scuffed pointed toes of Pee Wee's cowboy boots. Flames of fire are reflected in his boots. Or are they painted there?

"There are people who get a kick out of starting fires," he says. "There's a word for it—some kind of maniac. Fire-o-maniac or something like that."

"Pyromaniac," I say, feeling kind of proud of my vocabulary.

"Fool!" Mama spits at Pee Wee. She doesn't seem to have noticed my arrival. "Do you think you're scaring me? Do you think I'm afraid of fire? I am afraid of nothing."

I've always known Mama doesn't care much for Pee Wee,

THE TICKET

especially since the lottery win. But, still, this seems downright rude. Of course, Mama doesn't know what Pee Wee did at the tennis court, and he does seem kind of menacing today.

"You see that spider?" Mama points to a spider crawling up the calf of her leg. "Is he with you? He is, isn't he?" Then, in response to Pee Wee's perplexed expression, she laughs as if she's made the cleverest joke ever. "I'm not afraid of that spider. In fact, I think he's afraid of me."

I lean over, brush the spider off Mama's leg. "You never know," I say, "it might be one of the poisonous kinds."

She's behaving so peculiarly, I only want to escape. "Lori's dad is picking me up in a few minutes," I tell her. "Remember, you said I could spend the night?"

She says nothing, which I take to mean okay. I feel sort of uneasy about the way she's acting, but Gram should be home soon. Gram has started going on afternoon walks, but they don't last long. Constitutionals, she calls them.

"If the house—your house—was to burn down," Pee Wee says softly, as if talking to himself, "what would that do for us—for you and me? Old Jesse would have to buy a new house, wouldn't he? A better house, a bigger house . . ." His voice trails off, as if he's reconsidering the idea. I think again of the way Pee Wee saved me at the tennis court, and it occurs to me that he and Mama have some things in common. It's like they both have two personalities, a Jekyll and a Hyde.

Mama picks up his train of thought, suddenly animated and talking rapidly. "You know, I've been thinking that the house needs a complete remodeling. But a *new* house would be better still, a house with all the latest conveniences in an upscale neighborhood, the sort of house we deserve. Don't you think so, Tray?"

So she does know I'm here. I can't decide which of the pair of them is weirder today. "I suppose so," I say. "Well, I'll see you later." I hurry inside to get my stuff together.

CHAPTER TWENTY-ONE

I'M AT LORI's when I hear. The call comes from Dad, who sounds as stunned as I feel. I drop the phone and tear out of the house.

Voices call after me.

"Tray! What is it?" It's Lori, urgent to stop me from running. But I cannot be stopped.

"I could drive you." Lori's father's voice booms loudly, and the offer makes me hesitate for a second. But I know how he moves, slow as molasses. I cannot bear to wait for him to do whatever he would need to do—change his shoes, or locate his keys, or whatever. So I wave my hand and keep on running.

The few blocks from Lori's house to mine seem endless. I hear the sirens, terrifying in their shrill message, and I remember now that I have been hearing them for some time, even before the phone call. I had paid no attention. I have often laughed at Gram, who always worries about me whenever she hears the sound of a siren. Unless, of course, I am with her. And if I am there, she worries about others who aren't.

"Why do you always imagine the worst?" I asked once, when Gram heard a siren and tracked me down at Lori's to make sure I was okay.

"I don't know," she'd admitted. "Can't help it, they give me this awful feeling."

Gram's image floats before me, vivid in its details. The

THE TICKET

safety pin in the waist of her skirt, a small smudge of snuff at the corner of her mouth, the tenderness in the faded blue eyes. I pick up the pace. There's a blister on my right heel; I forgot to put a band-aid on it this morning. It hurts with every step, but I barely notice. My heart hammers against my ribs, and I cannot tell if the hammering is from the effort of the run or the terror of what I will find. Even before I round the last corner, I smell smoke and see a plume of charcoal rising skyward. Then I'm around the corner, and I freeze. The house is gone. In its place, a mountainous dragon breathes coral fire, and black coils of smoke spiral like snakes.

Several fire trucks are parked nearby, and I wonder what purpose they have served, letting the house vanish like that, gobbled whole by the monster. In the next breath I am moving again, gasping, "Mama! Grammy! Where's Grammy?"

I push through the crowd of gazers, toward the front where a frowning police officer is trying to keep people behind an invisible line. I push past him—toward the dragon, toward the reptiles. *I am so scared . . . I am terrified of what I'm going to find out.*

"Stop that girl!" someone calls out, and I am pulled back, my arms pinned behind me, an angry voice in my ear. "What's wrong with you? Are you trying to get yourself killed?" The speaker's face is flushed with the heat, and I am hot now, too. My eyes sting from the smoke and I rub them with a fist, surprised to find that my face is wet. I don't remember crying.

I say nothing, cannot find words. There are people around me, unfamiliar faces—who *are* they?—neighbors I don't know, or curious passers-by, drawn to the scene of tragedy. A myriad of voices drift toward me. One shrill female voice rises above the others. "They say the woman started it herself."

"What? For the insurance?"

"No, I don't think so. She's crazy, they say. Has a history of acting peculiarly. And, besides, her husband just won the lottery."

"I heard that somebody saw a suspicious-looking man pedaling away on a bicycle. They say it was that fellow who claimed he bought the ticket."

"No, I heard it's a kitchen fire. Most likely it was an accident."

"Not what I heard—I heard it started in the garage, and the police are already looking for the man who bought the ticket, the one on TV."

"Who was inside when it happened?" someone inquires, and I strain to hear the reply.

"The old woman and the younger one, too, I think. Frank said there were two bodies being hauled out when he got here."

The faces around me are starting to swim before my eyes, and I think I may faint. Frantically, I look around me, seeking my dad's face in the crowd. Or Gram's. I want her to be here to comfort me, to make everything all right the way she always has. To tell me it's a mistake. The vise gripping my chest is so tight I can't breathe, and it occurs to me that I might be having a heart attack. *Where is Grammy?*

No one is holding me now, and I can slip away. But I stand rooted because I don't know where to go. And still the voices go on. "Yeah, I was here before Frank. I came in right behind the fire trucks, and the women were just coming out the door. You wouldn't believe—the old woman was on fire, her clothes all ate up in flames, and she was pushing the younger one out in front of her, and then the porch just collapsed on top of her. The younger one was kicking and screaming, all crazy-like, when the firemen got to them."

"I saw it, too," another voice chimes in. "She was screaming something about a prowler. Said she knew who did it, wanted to find him and make him pay."

"Who?"

"The crazy one. And then the next minute she was saying how she had to do it, how it was the only way and to please just let her go back in, please let her die."

I let out a small choking sound, struggling to breathe, feeling the space and the heat and horror closing in on me. Someone notices me then. "Shh. I think that's the girl. The one that lives here."

THE TICKET

I look into a pair of kind eyes, old, sad eyes, and they are familiar. My brain is numb, and I cannot place the eyes or the face. "Here, child," the man says. He pulls a handkerchief from his pocket and dabs at my face. "Is this your house?"

I recognize the voice. It's the old man on the corner, the one who lives alone and always gives me the best Halloween candy, who always bought boxes of cookies or candy from me when I had to sell stuff for school. How normal my life had been then, and I hadn't appreciated it. It will never be like that again. I can see this as clearly as if it were written in the sky, a message curling itself out of the smoke, a message from God. I am being punished for my string of sins: self-centeredness, greed, lack of compassion . . . the list goes on and on.

"Officer!" the man calls, and I cringe, start to pull away. "Don't," he says gently, "I just thought we'd try to get you some help, you know, find out where they are and everything."

I want to scream and cry and collapse. I want it to be a dream. I want it all to go away. Instead, I let the old man lead me to the edge of the crowd, where he speaks quietly to a policeman.

The policeman turns to me. "Where's your daddy?"

"I don't know." I try to think. "He called me, but I haven't seen him since I got here."

"He's probably already at the hospital," the uniformed officer says. He, too, has kind eyes, light brown with puffy bags under them. "I'll take you there, okay?"

"Yes, please." I swallow, praying that if I'm polite, if I behave, then maybe Mama and Gram will live.

"Don't worry. We'll get the man who did this," the officer says.

I cannot answer. There's an enormous lump in my throat, and I can only wonder how it matters who did it or whether they get the person. If it's done, it's done.

I sit in the back of the squad car saying nothing. I bite the cuticles of my fingers until they bleed, remembering my most recent mean words to Gram and imagining life without her, with only a hole where she should be.

"Is that what you're worried about—whether you can forgive

yourself?" I'd said, or something like that. And another time: "You don't understand! You don't understand *anything!*" What horrible, ugly lies, when all along I knew Gram was the only one who had ever understood me, the only one who cared enough to *try* to understand.

"Please, God, I'm so sorry," I sob into my hands. "Please let her live so I can tell her."

THE TICKET

CHAPTER TWENTY-TWO

THE DAY OF Gram's funeral dawns bright and sunny and beautiful, yet horrible because Gram cannot see it, will never see it or anything else ever again. It is unseasonably warm, or maybe not. Perhaps, instead, the weather has been unseasonably cold earlier in the year. I seem to remember hearing Gram say something to that effect. Today may simply be a return to normal temperatures. I don't know and I don't care. I have never cared about the weather. Weather is something grownups discuss, as though it has importance when it has none. Yet here I am, in the middle of Gram's funeral, thinking of the weather.

I glance at my mother. She's been in the hospital since it all happened, so I wasn't really expecting her at the funeral. I guess they let her out for the festivities. She's surprisingly calm. She dabs at the corner of one eye with an embroidered handkerchief, but her eyes look perfectly dry. Like mine. Maybe when the hurt is too deep, your eyes forget how to cry. Mama's eyes aren't just dry; they are glazed over, as if she's somewhere else. They probably have her on some potent drugs. At least she's alive, which is more than she deserves. I feel mean to be thinking this way. It would be worse, *of course, it would*, if she and Gram were both dead. (*Yet how could it be worse?*)

It's hard to think of this ceremony as being for Gram when Gram cannot hear a single word said, when her body lies cold and

THE TICKET

vacant inside a metal box. I hear my name and jerk to attention. "... for her granddaughter, Tray," the preacher has said. What was the first part of the sentence? I try to fill in the blanks—*her selfless devotion* for her granddaughter, Tray, or *her constant presence* for her granddaughter, Tray, or *her unreciprocated love and affection* for her granddaughter, Tray? It seems of vital importance in this moment to know, to figure it out. Later, if I ask someone, even the preacher himself, he will stare at me blankly. Blank, the way Mama looks. Blank, the way I feel without Gram. *What could this man possibly know about my relationship with Gram?*

Could Gram have confided in him? Of course, she *could* have. She spoke of him often enough to me—maybe she also spoke of me to him. Gram was never ashamed to speak of her love or her pride in me. But did I reciprocate? No. Not once can I remember saying, "I'm proud of you too." Or "I'm proud to have you for my grandmother." It seemed unnecessary. Somehow, stupidly, I never really expected anything to change, so I acted like the opportunities—to tell Gram how I feel, how sorry I am—would always be there.

In my foolish head, I would always be fourteen; Gram would always be my Gram, had always been an old woman, and when she talked about *someday*, I had no patience at all. Now I'm remembering all the years with Gram before I was fourteen and seeing all the years ahead without her. I'm remembering Gram saying that someday I would know I am exceptional and so would everyone else. Nobody ever believed this about me except Gram, and now Gram is gone.

I lift my knotted fist to my mouth and bite the skin on my knuckle hard so that, for a moment, this fresh pain blocks out the ache in my head and my heart, and the constant dull throbbing from my period. Years from now, will I remember I was having my first period on the day of Gram's funeral? I need to tell Gram, and it breaks my heart that I can't.

One day, when I was eleven, Gram had come into my bedroom unexpectedly. "It's time you got prepared for something special that's going to happen to you. Maybe soon, maybe not for a few years." Gram's forehead arranged itself into the map of lines that meant she was worried about something. About my reaction, for instance.

My excitement at the words "something special" evaporated, replaced by a sense of anxiety, the way I felt when the teacher announced a pop quiz and I wasn't prepared. "What?"

"You're going to become a woman, and that means certain changes to your body." Gram's face reddened a little, and I could feel an answering flush in my own cheeks.

I noticed a pink box clutched to Gram's chest. "What's that?"

It was a box of Kotex, dainty ones with pink stripes, and a pamphlet inside that described the changes, with drawings to illustrate. "It's a beautiful thing, actually," Gram said, and I'd shrugged, acting disinterested.

In private, though, I read the brochure over and over until I knew it by heart. Anxious for the event, I examined my panties daily for traces of blood. Once I spotted a bit of red fuzz or thread, and actually wore a Kotex for a full day before giving up on it. It was Gram who convinced me to relax and not be in such a hurry. Somehow Gram had managed to make me look forward to something that might otherwise have scared me to death—just as Gram later told me that sex can be a beautiful thing.

And, because Gram says it, I know it is true. I don't want to think of Gram in the past tense. Still, I can't fully picture her face in my mind, and this failure horrifies me. If she is already fading, how can I hope to hold her in my mind and heart forever—like she said I would?

More than anything in the world, I want it back—the time before all this. If only I hadn't been at Lori's that day, I know I could have saved Gram. Somehow. It's my fault, my own selfish fault. Mine and Evelyn's.

I look at her again. I barely recognize the cool, self-possessed (if somewhat dazed) woman who is my mother. Everyone has been commenting on how well Evelyn is holding up *under the circumstances*. The words are uttered in hushed tones, like a deep, dark secret. But I know what they mean. Some of them think

THE TICKET

Evelyn started the fire, that Evelyn killed her own mother. The police don't think so, though.

They have Pee Wee Johnson in custody.

I want to believe Pee Wee did it because the alternative is too awful. I see Pee Wee's face suddenly, his hair standing out about his baseball cap, his eyes concerned. Concerned for me, angry too, that day at the tennis court. I've told no one but Gram. Although the incident had nothing to do with the fire, somehow I know Pee Wee did not start it. And with that knowledge comes a powerful surge of emotion.

I hate my mother with a ferocity that shakes me. But I am frightened for her, also. There is something not right about her calm, something altogether unnatural. I don't want to think about it. I want to feel only hatred for her so I won't have to hate myself. For an instant, I hate Gram, too, for leaving me to deal with this crazy family alone. I have no one now.

The most inappropriate thought comes to mind. Rodney has not called as he said he would. Not that I care anymore. Maybe he doesn't know how to find me, since I'm staying with Lori. Or maybe he thinks I'm too absorbed by everything that's happened to care about school stuff. Perhaps he has simply forgotten. *What is wrong with me?* I cannot *believe* I am sitting here thinking about Rodney at a time like this, when I should be thinking only of Gram, and how wrong I've been about everything. Nothing stays the same. Everything changes and I was stupid to long for change. Now I just want to hold on to the past, to the childish belief that things can go on forever.

Of course, I've always known that girls become women and then old women and that old women die, but none of this has ever been real to me before. If I concentrate as hard as I can, can I see Gram's face? Not as it looks in the coffin, but as it looked in life?

The lines around her mouth, the mole on her nose, the smudge of a snuff stain, the eyes brimming with life. I want to see Gram's face, the way it appears when that faraway look comes into her pale eyes, when she launches into stories about her past.

Like when she met Grampa, or even the sad stories about things she did wrong, or thought she did wrong. I resolve if I could just hear them one more time, *this* time I would be sympathetic; this time I would reassure Gram instead of taunting her.

Out of nowhere, I see Gram clear as day. I see her singing along with Rod Stewart. Which song was it? *Mandolin Wind?* No. *Maggie May*. Gram's voice is cracking on the high notes, and she and I are laughing together. And now my eyes are no longer dry. I am crying out loud, forgetting for the moment where I am, that I am not alone. The sound of my sobs draws sympathetic looks from the people around me. From all but my mother. Her eyes meet mine; they are as blank as a freshly erased blackboard.

I stifle my sobs. After *Maggie May* had ended that day, the next song on the radio was "You're No Good." I know this to be true. Gram always thought I was good. Gram always believed in me, but Gram was so wrong! I want to scream out the lyrics.

I'm no good . . . I'm no good . . . I'm no good. Baby, I'm no goo-od . . .

I have to get a grip. Gram would want me to behave in a dignified fashion today, and I owe her that much. But the other memories are coming after me, the ones I want to forget, the ones I want to erase forever. Why did I get so angry with Gram? What trivial thing would drive me time and again to the point of saying horribly irretrievable things to the only person in my world who ever really loved me?

It had to do with me, of course, with my fears. It was always about me. Selfish, oh, so selfish. I bite my knuckles again, but this time the pain in my stupid, selfish body cannot blot out the other, deeper pain. The memories are pouring down now, like a hard rain. A flood of memories. The bad ones are so bitingly sharp, and they keep coming, playing over and over. Really, it wasn't so bad, I want to argue, but the memories say otherwise.

All I'd wanted was for Gram to tell me that I could never, *ever* inherit my mother's condition. Instead, Gram threw out one of her usual clichés, something about not crossing bridges until you get there. How was I to know it was the *last* time I'd ever

THE TICKET

hear Gram speak those words? But somehow I know that, in the future, when the occasion calls for one of Gram's clichés, it will automatically come to me.

What I don't know is whether I will eventually erase the hateful words I spoke that day. *"Then why did you tell me all this? What were you thinking?"* I'd flung out the words and then voiced the cruelest thing I could think of. *"I may not have any crazy genes at all, but now that you've shared all these stories about your mother with me, I'll never be sure, will I? I'll never be able to have a baby without being afraid. Thanks, Gram. Thanks a lot!"*

Someone nudges me now, and I look up. Dad motions for me to rise, to follow him to take one last look at Gram's body. He takes my hand. I flinch, and he drops it.

I have to be alone when I say goodbye.

Gram looks beautiful. Her eyes are closed, and her lips are a soft coral, not quite smiling but peaceful. Strange, that she looks beautiful to me now when I have never thought of her that way before. Not as beautiful. Not as anything, really, except old. Once a worker at our house—someone patching the roof, I think—told me I looked like my grandmother. I acted insulted, in spite of Gram's presence nearby.

"What? You don't want to look like your grandmother?" the man said, sounding surprised. It didn't occur to me at the time that the man might have been flirting with Gram, that she was capable of drawing male attention in that way.

"I don't want to look like any old woman," I told him. Gram repeated the story to the rest of the family. She seemed amused, but I wonder. Did I hurt her feelings that day, too?

"Oh, Gram," I say to the beautiful body in the cold coffin. "I hope I will look like you someday." For the first time, I can see clearly the body and soul of the young woman inside my grandmother that I sometimes glimpsed for a fleeting instant, but could never quite hold while she lived. It is as if the years have melted away inside the coffin.

The choir is singing softly. *"Gather with the saints at the river that flows by the throne of God."* They have been singing for some time, but I just now hear them. I remember Gram with her worn Bible in her lap—her skirt safety-pinned at the waist. Quoting scriptures that I only half listened to. Promising to pray about things that bothered me. The singers sound like angels, welcoming my grandmother home to heaven.

They are singing another song now; one I have heard Gram sing a hundred times. *"Some glad morning when this life is o'er, I'll fly away; to a home on God's celestial shore, I'll fly away. I'll fly away, fly away, oh glory, I'll fly away. When I die, hallelujah, by and by, I'll fly away."*

THE TICKET

CHAPTER TWENTY-THREE

The hours creep past so slowly that the days after Gram's funeral seem more like a season than a week. Nothing in my life will ever feel right again. It certainly doesn't feel right for me to be here in Lori's house. Dad's staying in a motel, but he thought I'd be better off here. I thought so too, at first. Now I wonder.

It's not so much that I feel like an intruder, which I do, or that they aren't nice enough to me, which they are (most of the time). It's just not *home*. Besides that, I am learning way more about Lori's family than I really want to know. It was one thing for Lori to tell me about their problems, and altogether another to see them firsthand.

I've learned, for instance, that what happened the day we went shopping with Lori's mother—when Julia piled up the purchases and then walked away without them—isn't all that unusual. I've learned that Lori's dad sometimes drinks a lot, and that Julia nags him about it. I've learned that he has a nasty temper when he drinks, and that Julia's spending too much can drive him to the point of screaming and kicking holes in the walls. I've learned that screaming at each other is a way of life in some families.

"Why do you do this to me?" he explodes at Julia one morning, just when I am trying to swallow a bit of oatmeal, which turns immediately to glue in my mouth.

"Why do you think everything is about you?" Julia asks, her

voice quieter, but no less venomous, than her husband's. "Did it ever occur to you that if you were a better provider for your family, I might be able to enter a few stores in town without being chased out like a housefly?"

"Ha!" he snorts. "I'd like to *see* the provider who could keep up with your spending. If you think you can find one, feel free—" He drops into an exaggerated bow and sweeps one arm in a broad arc, like a speaker introducing a princess at a ball. *"Be my guest."*

Julia glances in my direction and shoots a warning glare at her husband. At moments like this, they act inhibited by my presence, as if I've only just materialized in the room. When this happens, I want nothing more than to vanish, like the ghost I've become. At other times, they get so caught up in their quarrel, they are oblivious. I don't know which is worse.

I gulp a sip of orange juice and move as inconspicuously as I can manage to the sink. I rake the sticky contents of my bowl into the side with the garbage disposal, rinse out the bowl and glass, place them in the dishwasher, and make my escape. I can feel their eyes on my back, but by the time I reach the hallway, their voices rise again.

Despite all this craziness, Lori somehow remains calm. She is the strong one. Funny how I believed for a time that I was the stronger of us two; that Lori needed me. I know now the opposite is true. "I don't know how you do it," I say.

"Do what?"

"Stay so—so normal. So calm when all this is going on."

"What choice do I have?" Lori twists a strand of honey-colored hair around her finger.

"I think I'd be tempted to get in the middle of it—to scream and take sides or something."

"Whose side would you take?"

I stare at Lori's outfit while I think how to answer. She's wearing a new pair of bell-bottom jeans with a soft-brown leather belt and a crisp white long-sleeved shirt with a big button-down collar. I once would have given anything for an outfit like that, but I don't feel even a twinge of envy now. As much as I like Julia,

I also understand Lori's father's helpless rage. "I don't know," I admit.

"Maybe that's how. I love them both, even though I want to kill them half the time."

I am quiet, thinking of Gram and Mama.

"I'm sorry," Lori says quickly. "I wasn't thinking. I didn't really mean that." It takes me a second to figure out what Lori's sorry for. Just a careless remark . . . I wonder if it will always be like this, with people stumbling over their words around me.

"I know," I say, trying to stop the stupid tears I feel sliding down my cheeks. "It's all right." Uncharacteristically, Lori reaches over to hug me, and I lean down to bury my tear-stained face in my much shorter friend's shoulder. *Why does there have to be so much unpleasantness to stumble over?*

"There are some questions about the insurance," Dad had said to Lori's father when he dropped me off.

"Aren't there always? One thing about insurance companies is they'll deny if they can find any excuse," Lori's dad said. Then his face reddened, probably because he just remembered that Dad is in the insurance business.

Another time, Julia had apologized to me after a screaming bout, her face strained and sad. "I'm sorry you had to witness that."

"It's all right," I said.

But it wasn't. Nothing is all right, and it really doesn't help to know Lori's life isn't so perfect either. Maybe I've wanted to believe that, in other families, things are better, with everyone communicating and smiling at each other like on *The Waltons* or *Little House on the Prairie*.

Today, I'm sweating under Julia's worried gaze. "My dad's coming to pick me up for dinner," I say, to explain why I am hovering near the front door.

"That's nice," Julia mumbles and moves away.

I still like Julia, but I pity her, too, and that makes me uncomfortable around the woman. I decide to step outside to wait. A neighbor's dog barks, and I call to him. "Here, pup!" I

─── THE TICKET ───

pat my thighs, and he heads in my direction. A chain jerks him back, a chain I had not noticed until now, and I feel a sharp flash of affinity.

The fresh outdoor air is a relief. I suck it in. Lori's house is always so warm. I guess I sort of got used to Dad's habit of keeping the house a little cool in the cooler months, like now, and a little on the warm side during the heat of summer. Sometimes, forgetting our house no longer stands, I head in that direction before memory strikes, and I have to return to the stifling heat of Lori's. Even Lori's collections—that include an *amazing* number of record albums in comparison to my meager few that got destroyed in the fire—do not make up for the heat.

Or for the outbursts.

There is a restlessness inside me, a restlessness that has little to do with the heat or stale air. It has to do with Pee Wee Johnson and the incident at the tennis court, with what I know but have confided to no adult. No one but Gram, who cannot tell. I know, like I know my name, this restlessness has to do with the fire and how I'm almost positive Pee Wee didn't start it. And with my fear that he'll be blamed for it, regardless of whether he's guilty or not.

Dad's car pulls into the driveway, and I rush over, anxious to hear his plans. Surely tonight he's going to tell me he's come to take me away from here . . . take me with him somewhere, *anywhere*. Once I'm away from here, just maybe the restlessness will abate.

"Where would you like to go for dinner?" he asks.

"I don't know. Surprise me."

But Dad seems incapable of making a decision, and finally I'm the one who chooses Long John Silver's. I wait, over fried shrimp, for him to tell me where we're going to live, but he is silent as a doorpost. I stare at him, willing him to talk to me. He absently dips a shrimp in cocktail sauce before biting into it.

Finally, I ask, "Are we going to rebuild the house? Or look for another one?"

"I don't know." He dabs his mouth with a paper napkin. "I've been so busy with the arrangements and all."

"What arrangements?"

"You know. The funeral—your mother—the insurance—everything."

"I see." I do see, but I am disappointed, sorely disappointed. I have so needed him to take charge, and clearly he has no intention of taking charge of anything. He is just going to deal with things as they force themselves upon him.

Over Dad's shoulder, I see a young couple teasing each other, the woman playfully feeding a French fry to the man; a family with a baby in a highchair and two older kids exploding with laughter when the baby misses his mouth and smears chocolate pudding all over his face; an elderly couple reaching across the table to hold hands. But right now I'm too racked with pain and anxiety to feel anything but jealousy. Jealousy for what they all have, and I do not. How inconsistent I am, disappointed one minute because Lori's family is troubled, and jealous the next because these people seem happy.

"Am I going to stay at Lori's forever?" I say, trying to bury my fear under sarcasm, and then the appalling thought strikes that perhaps the idea is not as ludicrous as I imagined.

"No, of course not. Just for . . . for now."

I wait for him to ask me if I like it there, but he doesn't. I am sullen for the remainder of the evening, silently challenging him to ask me what's wrong.

But he's too preoccupied to even notice, and his preoccupation drives me to speak up at last. "I hate it there, Dad! How long do you expect me to stay?"

For a moment, surprise flickers in the dull green eyes, and hope springs to life that maybe now that he knows how I feel, he will take action. But the hope is short-lived, as he just pats my hand. "I'm sorry, Tray, but there's not much I can do. At least this way you won't have to miss any school."

Who cares about school? I want to shout. I say nothing, a new hopelessness crushing every pore of my body, including my mouth. When he drops me back at Lori's house, my feet are so heavy I can barely pick them up to walk.

"Someone called for you," Lori says, as soon as I'm inside.

"Who?" My pounding heart tells me now that hope isn't quite dead, after all.

"Guess!"

"Rodney?"

"Yes!"

"What did he say?"

"Just for you to call him back."

Fingers trembling, I misdial the first time and have to start over. When he answers, and we get past the hellos and how-are-you's, he asks me if I want to get together to review for the next test.

"To review for the next test?" I repeat, like a slow-witted parrot. "Sure, I'd love to get together. Where?" I pray he doesn't say we can meet at Lori's. Another thing I have learned about Lori's family is there is no privacy whatsoever. Even now, Julia hovers like a moth. I glance at her. She smiles and I smile back, kind of absently, because I don't know what else to do.

"My house, I guess," he says. "Unless you want to meet over there?"

"No," I say, probably a little too quickly, too loudly.

"Would you like for my dad to pick you up?" he asks.

I glance at Julia, who is now pretending to look at something outside the window. "Yes . . . if it isn't too much trouble."

"The only question now," Lori says when I tell her, "is what are you going to wear?"

My heart sinks at the thought. "I don't have anything nice."

"Why don't you try on some of my stuff?"

I shoot her a look that says in no uncertain terms: look at my arms and legs, and look at yours. Still, I agree, and for the next hour or so, we try one outfit after another. Most of them send us into spasms of giggles.

When we're about to give up, Lori pulls one last skirt from her closet. It's a pleated red and navy plaid wrap-around with fringe on the edge and a large brass safety pin, which is more for decoration than utility but which also serves to hold the fabric in place.

I hold my breath, hoping the waist will button easily. It does. It's much shorter on me, of course, but short skirts are in style.

"Is it *too* short?"

"Not at all," Lori says admiringly. "Your legs look really pretty. I wish mine were that long."

"No, you don't."

Lori's rummaging through a drawer now and doesn't argue. "Here, try this with it."

She hands me a blood red knit top with a turtleneck and three-quarter sleeves. I look at it doubtfully. It snaps at the crotch to give the bodice a smooth fit, but this means it will be way too small, and either won't snap or will snap open at the worst possible time.

"Go ahead, try it!" Lori urges.

Reluctantly I take the bodysuit. To my surprise, the fabric stretches so that it snaps easily and comfortably. "How do I look?"

"Gorgeous!" Lori says. "It never looked that good on me."

Pirouetting in front of Lori's full-length mirror, I'm not displeased with what I see. The skirt's shorter than I would prefer, but at least it's pleated so that it won't ride up when I sit. The bodysuit gives no indication of popping unsnapped, and the three-quarter sleeves disguise the fact that my arms are too long for the top. "Is this supposed to have three-quarter sleeves?" I ask suddenly.

Lori giggles. "Does it matter?"

"I suppose not. But what if I stretch it out so you can never wear it again?"

Lori shrugs. "I never wore it much anyway. Not a great color on me."

So it's decided. I'll have to wear my own jacket as the sleeves on any of Lori's would be way too short. But that's okay. I'm humming a little with pleasure at looking almost pretty for the date—I blush at the word "date" and search for one more appropriate to use for the occasion, even if only inside my head.

THE TICKET

CHAPTER TWENTY-FOUR

THE NEXT DAY, wedged in the front seat of a new-looking black car between Rodney and his father, I stifle a nervous giggle at the resemblance between the two male Irvines. Rodney's father's hair is red, like Rodney's, but a little thin on top. Not in a bad way, though, not ugly or anything. There's a curve to his mouth, too, which reminds me of Rodney, but with creases at the sides. It is as if I'm glimpsing what Rodney will look like when he gets old. Not exactly old, just older. Rodney's dad looks to be about the same age as mine, just not so tired or worn down. Pretty handsome actually.

Nobody's talking, and I try to think of something to say. The only thing that comes to mind is, "You really took after your son, didn't you?" It feels that way since Rodney came into my world first. But I stop myself, afraid they wouldn't be amused.

I am acutely aware of the warmth of Rodney's thigh through his jeans when it occasionally presses mine. Uncertain whether I leaned into him or him into me, I stiffen and withdraw my leg slightly. Immediately I miss the warmth and hope he doesn't feel rebuffed. My heart hammers so loudly, I wonder if Rodney's father can hear.

"Nice Corvette," Rodney remarks. His chin juts toward the windshield; his eyes scan the cars in the other lane. "Seventy-one?"

THE TICKET

"Seventy," his father says.

I turn my head to look at the cars we just passed, but I don't know which one he's talking about. For the first time ever, I wish I knew more about car makes and models. Apparently Mr. Irvine knows exactly which one Rodney is referring to.

"I can't wait 'til I get my license," Rodney says to me. "I'm gonna drive one of those."

"Sure, you are," his dad says with a chuckle. "More likely a Chevette if I was a gambling man."

"I'm going to save up for it."

"Lots of luck. You should have started when you were about two if you wanted to buy one of those babies."

I don't think I like Rodney's father. He should be encouraging Rodney to work toward his dream, not *dis*couraging him. "How much would it cost?" I venture.

"Depends," he says.

"What do you mean?"

"Depends on what features you want on it, whether you buy it new or used, stuff like that. Anywhere from twelve thousand to thirty thousand, I imagine. Like my dad used to tell me—let your pocketbook be your guide."

"I think it's admirable to have a goal," I say. "Don't you?" I am a little surprised at myself for speaking up in Rodney's defense.

"Depends on what the goal is." Mr. Irvine glances in my direction. At least he is talking to us now, I think, but I'm still not sure I like him.

Later, while I'm looking around the family den, I reconsider, like I'm falling in love with the whole Irvine family. First of all, the entire house smells so good, even the den; a sweet, yeasty smell like something is baking in the oven. There are framed shots on the walls of Rodney at all ages, of him rough-housing with his dad, of his sisters in cheerleading costumes when they were too little to be real cheerleaders. Several of all of them smiling in a studio setting.

Mixed in with the photos are a few plaques with Bible verses or poems. I scan them, trying not to think of Gram.

"Is that you?" I point to a photo of a chubby-faced baby in a sailor suit.

"Afraid so. I don't know why my mom keeps so many pictures all over the place. It's embarrassing."

"I like them," I say. "It's like the history of your family is on the walls." I think of my family. Mama lost interest in photos years ago, maybe when she realized I was getting too ugly to photograph. She was probably waiting for me to grow out of the ugly duckling stage, and I never did. Lori's family makes me want to cry, and now Rodney's family makes me want to cry, but for a different reason. My mother is crazy, my grandmother is gone, my father is indifferent, and I don't think there's a normal bone in my body. What can Rodney think of me? I need a cave to crawl into.

"Pretty boring stuff," Rodney says.

I look at the desk, an oak roll-top that looks like it might be an antique. "So you want to study some math?"

"Sure, if you do."

"Cookies anyone?" Rodney's mother enters, carrying a platter of hot chocolate chip cookies. The dark chocolate is melted slightly, just the way I love it. The cookies look warm and gooey and totally wonderful.

Rodney takes three cookies, and I take two. I want more, but don't want to be greedy. Rodney's mother smiles at us. "I'll just set these down here in case you want more." She clears a space on the corner of the desk and turns to go.

My mouth full, I feel the tears well up again.

"What's wrong?" Rodney says.

"Nothing," I mumble and try to swallow.

"Is it your grandmother?" Rodney asks.

"How did you know?"

"Just a lucky guess. I mean, not lucky. You know what I mean."

"She makes the best chocolate chip cookies," I say and then correct myself. "She *made* the best chocolate chip cookies." As I speak, I can feel a stinging in the back of my throat from the sobs that are threatening to erupt. I try hard to keep talking in a normal voice. I know I should steer away from the subject of Gram, but I can't seem to help myself. "Real big ones, with about twice as many chocolate chips as you're supposed to put in them. Sometimes she burned them, and sometimes they were a little raw, but I loved them any way she fixed them." On the last words, I lose the battle, and the sobs break out.

He pats my shoulder awkwardly. "I'm sorry," he says.

"I just can't believe she's really gone. Forever. I want it to be temporary, a stage I have to go through to learn about suffering or something. You know what I mean?"

Rodney nods, but I know he cannot possibly understand. I plod ahead anyway, no longer caring if Rodney will think I am strange or crazy, or too heavy-hearted to be any fun. "I keep wanting to go home and tell her things. Like that plaque over there. The one called *Footprints*." I point to it and Rodney follows the imaginary line from my finger. He makes no comment, just waits for me to go on.

"I want to ask her if she's ever read that poem. She was always sharing stuff like that with me. She had this calendar with stupid sayings on it. And she would always read them to me, but I didn't pay attention, not really. Now I miss them so much."

"Why don't you read them to yourself?" Rodney suggests.

"The calendar burned, remember?"

Rodney turns a faint shade of red, then recovers. "I bet we could find a calendar like it."

"It wouldn't be the same." I almost shout, frustrated at his lack of understanding. "*She's* the one who carried me when I was down. *She's* the one I need now."

"I know, I know," Rodney says. He pats my shoulder again, and this time his touch feels really good. I'm sorry I lashed out at him. I always seem to lash out at the wrong people.

I take a deep breath, trying to find the words to make him see. "I need to go home and tell her I'm sorry and bury my head in her lap. And sometimes, for a minute, I almost believe she'll be there. I want her to make all this mess right. She was the one who could always do that."

Rodney's hand is still on my shoulder; he's rubbing it around in circles. Circles upon circles, the way my thoughts keep spinning around and around and coming back to the same place without getting anywhere. The same place, the place that hurts the most.

"The thing is... I was so mean to her. Sometimes I complained about the cookies being burned, but I didn't really mind. *Why was I so mean?*" The tears leak out now.

"I bet she knew how you felt."

I rub at my eyes with my fists. "That's not the worst of it. I was so mean to her not long before she died, you wouldn't believe—I kept meaning to apologize, but I never did." *Why didn't I?*

"She probably knew that too, if she was as great as I think she was. From what you're telling me."

"But I was *so* horrid—I told her she was to blame for something that wasn't her fault, and it was the one thing that probably mattered to her more than anything else in the world." The conversation is flooding my head again, the conversation I will never, *ever* be able to escape.

I'll never be able to have a baby without being afraid. Thanks, Gram. Thanks a lot! If I ever do have a baby I won't be worrying about inherited diseases—I'll be wishing Gram was there to hold and love it.

Another time comes back to me, after the incident at the tennis court, when she wanted me to tell Dad and I didn't want to. What had I said that day?

Is that all you worry about—being able to forgive yourself? Oh, Gram! I didn't mean it. I never meant it at all.

Is it just me or is everybody the cruelest to the one person who gives them the most unconditional love? I suspect I treated Gram so badly because I took that love for granted—*do other people act in such a stupid, perverse way?* I want to ask Gram these things. Gram is the only one I could have asked. Rodney would never understand. He is way too normal.

His arm is completely around me now, and I am sobbing into his chest. I am sharply aware of his touch, his smell, his nearness. Through all the hurt and guilt, I am experiencing something

THE TICKET

new, and it feels amazing.

My sobs subside into hiccups, and I pull away. "I'm sorry to be such a baby," I say between hiccups.

"It's okay. Nobody could blame you."

He's wrong there: I blame myself. I don't feel in the mood to study math anymore. I do feel a little better for having cried, but I sort of want to be alone now. To process some stuff in my head. It's getting late too.

"I better call Julia—Lori's mom—to come get me."

"My dad can take you home."

"No, that's okay. Julia said if your dad was going to pick me up, the least she could do was bring me back." I don't add that Julia also said she wanted to get a look at where my new "boyfriend" lives. "So I guess I better be going. I'm afraid we didn't get much studying done."

"That's all right. We'll do better next time."

Next time? Is there going to be a next time?

When I start to place the call, Rodney's dad interrupts and positively insists on taking me home. On the way, he is practically chatty and I sort of get the impression he actually likes me, at least a little. My heart thumps its pleasure at this thought, and at the nearness of Rodney's thigh on the car seat next to mine.

CHAPTER TWENTY-FIVE

Lori's house is surprisingly quiet, almost hushed, when I slip in the door. I'm wishing I could be totally alone, like at home, to process the evening and relive every moment of tenderness. I pull the door shut as gently as possible, but not gently enough. Three voices call out to me.

"Tray!" That's Lori.

"Come in here," Lori's mother says.

"Hey, girl, we've got something to tell you." This from Lori's dad.

I follow the voices into the kitchen, where I find Lori's parents sitting companionably together, for once, their heads bent toward each other, their knees almost touching. A pitcher of tea sweats on the table and they each nurse a glass of melting ice cubes and watery tea. As usual, the house is way too warm for my taste.

They speak so softly, I can't catch a word, and then they turn as one toward me, their faces cheery. "I thought you were going to call me," Julia chides. She's wearing cream-colored wool slacks and a red cowl-necked sweater with a string of salt-water pearls. She looks chic as always.

"I was, but Rodney's dad insisted--"

"Never mind. That's not—"

Lori bursts into the kitchen, her eyes alight. "How was it?" she breathes. "Let's go to my room so you can tell me every little

THE TICKET

detail."

Lori deserves to be told, of course. Before I can follow her out, though, Julia addresses Lori. "Your father and I need to have a little private chat with Tray. You girls will have plenty of time together later."

Lori gnaws at her lip, and I know she wants to argue or to stay. She hesitates in the doorway, the toes of her copper leather boots pointed inward. At a significant frown from her dad, she shrugs and turns to go.

"We have some really good news," Julia says.

"Something we think will cheer you up," he adds.

At least they aren't planning to cross-examine me about my evening at Rodney's house, but what could it be? My mind races. Dad must have found us a place to live. A new house maybe. I try not to look overly eager. I don't want them to know just how anxious I am to get out of here. I bite my lip and wait.

"People all over town are talking about that man who started the fire at your house."

"Pee Wee?" I ask, knowing that of course it must be. Sweat has popped out above my lip, and I nervously lick it off.

"His real name seems to be Leonard Johnson, but, yes, it's the man called Pee Wee," Mr. Penman says. "He's been charged with murder. He's going to pay for what he did."

I'm so hot now I can't keep my jacket on another second. I shrug it off and sink into a chair, not wanting to hear but unable to keep from straining to catch every last word. "He'll get a fair trial, though, won't he?" I ask.

"There's not a woman or man in this town who doesn't know he's guilty. You don't have to worry that any jury around here will let him off," Julia says. She's trying to comfort me, I know, but accomplishing just the opposite.

"If they did, there would likely be a lynch mob waiting before he got home," Mr. Penman puts in, and I'm afraid they are both trying to read my expression. I fight to keep my face blank.

"I know it won't bring back your grandma," Julia says, and my eyes fill suddenly with unwanted tears. "But at least he'll pay for what he did. That's something."

But he didn't! I want to protest, but there's no point. They exchange puzzled looks. If I weren't so disappointed about this news, I might have been glad to see Lori's parents in such harmony.

"Thanks," I mutter and make my escape. Now I've got even more to process. Once again, I've descended in a matter of moments from such a hopeful high to a dismal low. But I've learned something. At least I think I have. It is that I am, and yet I'm not, like my mother.

Lori grabs me before I can reach "my room," which is a beautifully furnished guest room with a four-poster bed, yellow-and-blue ruffled curtains, and a matching bedspread, but which will never, ever, feel like *my* room.

We flop onto the bed in Lori's room, and I know how much she wants to hear about Rodney. But I haven't had time to figure it out for myself. And, right now, it simply is not my main concern.

"So?" Lori prompts.

I yawn. "I'm pretty tired, and it's getting late. I still need to study for that test."

"I thought that's what you were doing at Rodney's house," Lori says with a meaningful giggle. "Or didn't you two get any studying done?"

"Not much," I admit, but she can tell I'm distracted. This makes her think it went badly.

"What happened? Why are you so down?" She rolls over onto her side to peer at me.

"I'm not down," I say, hedging. "Aren't you going to ask me what your parents wanted to tell me so urgently?"

"Oh, that." Lori shrugs.

"You know?"

"Sure, I know. I don't know why they're acting like it's such a big secret." Lori rolls her eyes.

"But don't you see?" I'm surprised Lori is taking this so lightly. After all, she's the one person who knows what happened at the tennis court, how Pee Wee saved me.

"See what?" Her round eyes are puzzled.
"Pee Wee couldn't have started that fire."
"You said yourself he was creepy."
"Yeah, but that was before—" I break off.
"Before what?"

Lori can be so quick to catch on to what I'm thinking at times, and so agonizingly slow at others. Like now. I wonder if all relationships are like this. Just when you think someone understands you so well they can practically finish your sentences, all of a sudden you realize they don't get you at all.

When I say nothing, just shoot her a telling look, she finally figures it out. "I don't see what one thing has to do with the other. Everybody thinks he did it. Plenty of people have come forward saying they saw him lurking around your house." Now it's her turn to shoot me a sideways glance. "Besides, if he didn't do it, who did?"

"Maybe it was an accident. Not all fires get started on purpose, you know!" I can't tell her what I'm really thinking. As much as I want to, I just can't bring myself to say the words. So I tell her, instead, about my evening with Rodney.

CHAPTER TWENTY-SIX

When I make the call, my heart pounds so hard it fairly rattles my bones. By then, I have worked out the details of the lie, and I know I must stick to every single one of them . . . or be proven a fraud. I just want to give the police my story and be done with it. But the officer insists I come to the station to make an "official statement," whatever that is. This gives me ample opportunity to repent, to take back the words I'd forced out of my lying mouth. To admit the truth.

I squeeze my eyes shut and ask the question I've been dreading. "Um . . . can you tell me . . . will I need one of my parents there with me?"

There's silence on the other end of the line. Now I'm wishing I hadn't asked. Now I'm thinking the question makes me sound guilty. Which, of course, I am. I open my eyes slowly in wait.

"How old are you?" the voice asks.

"Fourteen."

"And you're just coming in to tell us what you saw?"

My stomach twists in knots. "Yes, sir."

"No. We don't need your parents here. If you were a suspect, it'd be a different story."

I breathe out. "No. Not me. I'm not a suspect." *Shut up, Tray. Shut. Up.*

"Can you get here on your own?"

THE TICKET

Brother. "No. There's no way I can get down there." A way out? Maybe.

"No problem. We'll send a car to come get you."

Maybe not.

Oh, Gram, what should I do?

I can hear Gram's answer as clearly as if she were here. "Pray about it," Gram says.

Oh, God, should I tell the truth? Is telling the truth an "always" rule, or are there exceptions? There have to be sometimes. And is this one of those times?

I wait for God's answer while I'm waiting for the police car. It's a small miracle I have managed to make this call and wait this long without being busted by Lori or Julia. Perhaps that in itself is God's answer.

I have left a brief note for them. *Don't worry. I'll be back soon.* Then I think better of the words "don't worry." Isn't that a clear invitation to worry? I wad up the paper, throw it in the trash, and rewrite the note. *Be back soon. Tray.*

The car comes, and I hop inside, heart hammering, palms sweating. I hope no one is watching through the window, or from the neighbors' houses, as the conspicuous-looking car pulls out of the driveway and down the street. No one except the dog who has become my friend and ally.

The two officers—both men, one tall, blond, and thin, the other balding and squatty—and I drive through town without a word between us. In the front seat, the police radio squawks a lot. I think it's kind of cool listening to the calls going back and forth. The 10-codes, I think they're called.

Once we arrive at the police department, the officers take me to an office past the main rooms filled with gray desks, square telephones, and stacks of files. The whole place smells of cigars and cold metal. We stop long enough for the officers to grab legal pads and paper.

"Follow us," the tall one says, without even looking my way.

Sure, I'm invisible. I'm your star witness, but I'm invisible.

I glance to the right and then to the left in the narrow hallway they're walking me down like I've done this every day of my life. I take in the framed pictures of officers receiving awards and plaques for shooting contests, alongside a couple of framed newspaper articles. I resist the temptation to straighten one that hangs crookedly, as out of place in the neat rows as I feel at this moment.

The door to the room is closed. While the tall officer opens it, my eyes focus on a plaque lined with brass plates honoring the names of fallen officers. There aren't many, but my stomach lurches. Fallen, like Gram, in the line of duty.

When we get in the room—which boasts a big gray-metal table with four chairs in the center, a long mirror on one wall, nothing on the other three—I sit where they tell me and start talking right away, as if my rambling will hush the butterflies fluttering around in my lying gut. "The thing is . . . I saw her that day before I left for Lori's." My voice quavers and I wonder if they can hear the lie in the quake. "She was messing around with the gasoline can in the garage, and I asked what she was doing. She acted funny, like I'd caught her at something. She said she just wanted to make sure there was enough. 'Enough for what?' I said. 'Enough in case . . . in case I run out,' she said. 'You know how your dad gets when I run out of gas.'" My feet tap in restless anticipation. Of what, I don't know.

The squatty officer tells me to slow down. He is busy flipping his pad open, trying to take notes fast enough to catch up. A quick glance over to the tall one and I see he is writing something too.

I take a breath and will myself to keep it sounding honest. With effort, I still my dancing feet. "Sorry," I mumble.

"Go ahead now," says the blond officer. I notice his eyes for the first time. They're kind, and when he speaks a deep dimple pops into one cheek.

"I thought that was strange," I say, my words coming slower, "because I don't remember her ever running out of gas. At least not in a long time. But she'd been acting so strange anyway, I didn't think too much about it. I thought she just liked the way

THE TICKET

it smelled, the way she was standing there inhaling it with this faraway look on her face." I'm starting to believe my own lie—I can actually see this happening—so maybe they will too.

The squatty officer frowns at me, his eyebrows forming a single dark line above his eyes. *It didn't work. He sees right through me*, I think, and I flush with shame mingled with something else. Relief? Fear? Can I be arrested for what I've done, I wonder. He didn't make me swear an oath, and I am a minor, so I'm thinking not.

Suddenly, to my embarrassment, I start to cry. My tears at least are genuine. *So genuine.*

Staring down, trying to think what to say, I focus on their hands. Squatty is—without my saying anything—writing new words on the long, yellow pad of paper before him. I try to read some of what's on the page from where I'm sitting. I see my words written there. My exact words. My damning words.

I think he believes me after all.

The backs of his hands are hairy, not a thick mat, but a noticeable one of straight, dark hair. Lifting my eyes, I see that his eyebrows nearly meet above the bridge of his nose, even though he's not frowning. With his balding head, he is like me. Not like tall and blond there, with his tanned skin and trim physique and adorable dimple. No, Squatty and I are bonded because we are two of the ugly ones.

I bet he has hair on his back too. I remember hearing some of the cheerleaders talking in the locker room one day about how disgusting they find this in men. *I could never, ever go to bed with a man with hair on his back*, one of them giggled, and the rest agreed.

He cannot help this, I know, any more than I can help my height. Nonetheless, I hope when I marry, my husband will not have dark hair on his hands and back, that he will be less like Squatty and more like Dimples. I sigh. Guess I'm just like everyone else, judging a person on the outside instead of the inside. Even this nameless stranger I haven't met yet. It dawns on me that I'm assuming I will actually find someone someday who wants to marry me . . . and that I *will* have some choice in the matter. Maybe Rodney. But probably not. Someone. I think of Julia's remarks about my height and my looks. And Gram's. Of course I never trusted Gram on the subject: she was way too biased. And Julia. She doesn't know anything (*does she know anything?*).

Maybe, just maybe, I'm not so ugly after all.

Squatty clears his throat, and I'm yanked back to the police interrogation room in a flash. I wonder if I will tell him—the man I marry—about this thing I am in the process of doing. Or will I keep the secret to my death? And if I tell him, will he understand?

He will not. He will think less of me because of this.

Now is the time. If I don't want this hanging over my head for the rest of my life, now is the time to come clean. The two men stare at me, pens poised, neither of them writing a word. They see I'm finished, and they collect their things.

Dimples tells me to wait in the room for a minute, then asks if I want a Coke® or something.

"No," I say, a little shy still in the presence of such gorgeousness. "But thank you."

He and Squatty stand and leave me to wonder if I'm about to be arrested. They know. I just know they know. They have secret ways of knowing. They are trained to read body language. One of my restless feet starts to tap out the beats of *Amazing Grace* at an accelerated tempo. My lips twist to the right. To the left. I scratch at an imaginary mosquito bite on my right shin.

The door opens and Dimples is back.

"Here you go, Tray." He produces a typed piece of official looking paper. "We just need your signature right here at the bottom."

He hands me a pen. A thin black one. I drop it onto the table, pick it up and giggle to say, "I'm such a klutz, can you believe it?"

I look from the paper to the officer to the door. I can stand up right now, I tell myself, and leave. Just walk out. Run out. I won't even need to say a word. I can find a phone, call Julia and ask her

THE TICKET

to come get me. It is *not* too late.

But then I think of Pee Wee, of his anger at the man at the tennis court, of my mother tossing garments frantically onto the floor, of her sitting at the kitchen table staring straight ahead.

I grip the pen and slide the paper closer to me. I pretend to read it when, in fact, every word on the page is blurry. When I sign the statement, my hand shakes so badly, my name is jagged. Fresh tears splash onto my signature, smudging the ink.

"Sorry," I whisper, sliding the paper back toward the officer without looking up.

The deed is done.

CHAPTER TWENTY-SEVEN

THE NEXT TIME Dad picks me up at Lori's, I brace myself for the visit. Don't expect too much, and you won't be disappointed, I tell myself. In fact, don't expect *anything*.

Sliding away from my dad, I think of the pervert at the tennis court and I wonder for the umpteenth time: would it have made a difference if I'd told Dad as Gram urged me to do? Every action or, in this case, inaction has an effect on the chain of events that follows. Something as simple and seemingly unrelated as my telling Dad about the pervert could have saved Gram, might have altered Mama's state of mind just enough to prevent her from doing what she did. What I *think* she did.

Just as I'd done on that day, I cling to the door.

"I've got a surprise for you," Dad announces.

"Oh? What?" Hope rises in spite of my effort to suppress it.

"If I told you, it wouldn't be a surprise, now would it?" Dad's voice is teasing, and he seems pleased with himself.

I hope, hope, hope it's a new house. I watch with interest as trees and houses and manicured lawns slide by. There is something familiar about this drive, something menacingly familiar.

Realization strikes, and I stifle a gasp. We're headed to the tennis courts. Has Dad somehow found out what happened here? I have a sinking feeling in the pit of my stomach, but Dad's

THE TICKET

countenance certainly doesn't look like he's on to me.

Ironic, I'd just been thinking about the fat man and about that day. And now this. Not really surprising, though, since it's never far from my thoughts. What's more surprising is the fact that Dad and I are here together.

It's a Saturday, a bit overcast though not raining. It's the first time I've been here since that day, and nausea floods my whole body, right down to my toes, at the memories. I fight it down. "What are we doing here, Dad?"

"That's the surprise!" He opens his door, jumps out with more energy than I've seen from him in a while, and fairly flies around to my side to open my door.

I follow him tentatively to the rear of the car, where he pops the trunk. Inside lay two new aluminum tennis rackets. They are beautiful, absolutely beautiful. He picks them up and hands one to me. I unzip the cover, which reads "prince" in green writing, except for the "i," which is in white and dotted with tennis balls. Dad is unzipping his "HEAD" racket; it's an Arthur Ashe.

"Wow!" I'm awestricken. My racket is so light, and the grip feels perfect. The old racket I'd been using, which belonged to Mama about a hundred years ago, was a wooden antique.

For a moment, my misgivings vanish, and I'm anxious to try it out. Dad lifts a can of brand-new tennis balls and opens it with a ping. The smell of the new balls assails my nostrils, and the nausea is back, only worse than before.

Bile rises in my throat and mouth, and I swallow it down, not wanting to yield to thoughts of the fat man and his tennis balls, not wanting Dad to know. "It's beautiful, Dad," I say, taking a ball and juggling it on the new lightweight racket.

"I thought maybe we could play together sometimes," Dad says, "if you'd humor your old man. The exercise would be good for me."

"Sure." But as I say it, the ghost of a shadow flickers across the backboard where the pervert practiced while he watched me.

There's no one here today but me and Dad. I have to get a grip. Dad glances at the sky. "I'm afraid it's going to rain, but maybe it will hold off for a while."

I deliberately skip a little as I head toward the baseline on the second court, the one with no hole in the net. I try not to look over my shoulder to see if anyone else is approaching. I register that no one has replaced the holey net yet.

Dad goes to the good net and performs a measurement with his racket. "We used to do this with the old wooden rackets," he explains, "to see if the net is the right height. But I'm not sure if it works with the new racket shape." He shrugs. "It looks about right."

While Dad heads to the opposite baseline, I practice tossing a ball up, bouncing it with my new racket, and pretending not to be as nervous as a cat. I'm not sure whether my nerves are due to fear that I'll disappoint Dad with my lack of finesse or something darker. Even though it's chilly, a cold sweat stings my armpits.

"Do you want to serve, or do you want me to?" Dad calls.

"You go ahead." I move toward the service line, not sure how far back to stand. I shift my weight from one leg to the other, crouch into a receiving pose like I know what I'm doing, then straighten up because I certainly do not. Dad tosses the ball high and serves it gently into the net. I suspect he's trying to take it easy on me.

"I'm pretty rusty," he apologizes, lifting his voice so I can hear.

"Go ahead and challenge me, Dad," I call back. "I'm so used to playing with Lori—it will be good for me to try to hit with somebody who's—" I bite back the word 'better,' not wanting to be disloyal to Lori, and finish with, "a bit more experienced."

He takes me at my word and serves a few hard ones. I can tell he's really good, or would be if he practiced, though several of them are just a little long. I'm able to return most of them, though, which pleases me immensely. "Why don't you serve a few?" Dad suggests.

I do, but I'm too nervous or else I'm just not used to the new racket yet. Several of them go into the wrong court, a few into the net, and only a couple into the correct service box. Even those are not nearly as fast as I'd like.

THE TICKET

"Keep practicing," Dad says. "The serve is the hardest part of the game when you're starting out."

The nausea that rises in my throat comes up so abruptly that I have to bend and retch. A thin stream of yellow vomit erupts from my mouth onto the concrete. Dad's words, I realize, are nearly the exact same words the fat man used one day, the day he told me I was looking good.

"What's wrong?" Dad says, coming around to my side of the court and removing a handkerchief from the pocket of his pants.

I dab at my mouth and hand the handkerchief back to Dad since I don't have any pockets. "It's just something I ate. Julia's oatmeal is nothing like Gram's, and it doesn't always agree with me."

It's true that the oatmeal is sitting badly in my stomach, but I'm still lying. There are sins of commission and sins of omission, Gram always said. I know I'm guilty of both kinds.

I glance toward the curb where our car is parked, just about a car's length in front of the spot where the fat man parked his that day. Suddenly, I can see him as clearly as if he were standing in front of me. Details I don't even remember noticing at the time. The dark hair on his knuckles, the raised veins in his neck, the broken blood vessels in the sides of his nose, the perfect fake-looking teeth, the smell of his breath.

The cold sweat drenches my shirt—neither Dad nor I are wearing great clothes for tennis—and I fight the impulse to vomit again. "You're white as a ghost," Dad says.

At the word, so apt for what I'm feeling and fearing, I can no longer keep it back. All the lies are making me sick. Thunder crackles as if God is trying to let me know where He stands on the subject of lying. I sink to my knees, and I heave and retch, and retch and heave, until nothing more comes out. Until I am emptied. I will never eat oatmeal again.

"Oh, Dad!" I bury my face in my hands. "I should have told you sooner."

"Told me what?"

I slide my hands under my thighs, which are trembling. I

force myself to meet Dad's eyes. "Pee Wee saved me. From this horrid man here, at the tennis court."

I can literally feel Dad freeze. All the reasons I didn't tell Dad in the first place seem unbearably trivial. "I can't help wondering if I'd told you sooner, maybe things would have turned out differently."

"What do you mean?"

What do I mean? Is there any way to articulate it without sounding crazy? "Everything might have been just different enough that—I don't know—that maybe it wouldn't have turned out the way it did."

He looks at me, and his eyes reveal a lack of comprehension. Then understanding dawns. "What happened to your gram, you mean." It's a statement, not a question. "Oh, Tray, don't blame yourself, don't even go there." Dad's voice has taken on a new firmness. "I need to know what happened to you here. Tell me everything."

I look down at my knees as I talk, and then I pull them to my chest and wrap my arms around my legs, avoiding Dad's eyes. When I finish, I steal a look at Dad to see that his hands are clenched white into fists. His face is a deep red, though, and I suspect my own is just as bright.

He doesn't speak for several long moments. When he does, his voice is very quiet. "You should have told me."

"I know!" I wail. "I was stupid and selfish, and I'm so, so sorry. I thought you'd keep me away from the tennis court if I told you, and I didn't want that to happen. But if I'd told you, maybe you could have kept Pee Wee out of jail and all that. Instead I—I—" I break off, unable to go on. Just when Dad and I are starting to get along with something akin to mutual respect—for the first time ever, maybe—I have to go and ruin it.

"What, Tray?"

I suck in an audible, shaky breath and my next words come out in a rush. "I told this awful lie about Mama. I told the police I saw her with the gas can. But I didn't. I lied! Oh, Dad, what kind of person would do something like that to her own mother?" I bury my face in my hands again, rocking back and forth.

THE TICKET

"A person who had been through something terrible. A person who was pretty mixed up. "A person who is trying to make things right."

I shiver and he pulls me against his side. His touch is at once rough and tender, and I know he's battling with conflicting emotions, as I have been for so long.

I nod, gulping now with the fluid that is flooding my nose, my eyes, my throat. "I just told them that so they'd let Pee Wee go—and—and they did. But now Mama's... Oh, Dad, *what have I done*?"

"The police were collecting a lot of evidence, Tray. What you told them was only one of a number of statements," he says. "The insurance company was able to establish where the fire started. And it was in the kitchen, not the garage. That's why they released Pee Wee. Not because of anything you said. And your mother is exactly where she needs to be, for now. To get the help she needs. When you're ready, we can go to the police and correct your statement. Tell them about the man at the tennis court, too."

I say nothing, not sure I'll ever be ready. I think back to the day I told the lie. I hadn't been ready then, either. It's starting to sprinkle, and Dad pulls me to my feet, grabs our new rackets, and hustles me to the car.

"What about our balls?" I ask.

"We can buy more."

We drive in silence for a time, absorbed in the comprehension of what has, at last, passed between us. When he speaks again, his voice is firm though quiet. Little more than a whisper really. "Tray, please, please don't keep important stuff like this from me *ever again*. Please, promise me."

"Okay." I draw a deep tremulous breath. "I promise."

Thunder crackles loudly, lightning flashes in front of us, and suddenly the rain is slapping the car, the windshield, the windows in quick erratic splashes, as if it too is infuriated by my deceit, letting me know that forgiveness is not that simple. It is likely to be a long time before I can completely forgive myself.

CHAPTER TWENTY-EIGHT

DAD GRIPS THE steering wheel as if it might escape. Rain continues to slap the windshield of the car, and I welcome the grayness of the sky, a sign of God's dark mood—it seems appropriate. I wait for Dad to speak, trying to imagine what he's feeling and thinking, what he's needing. I catch the shine of something glistening on his cheek, caught in the headlight of an oncoming car and then vanishing.

"It's just us now," he says at last. "You and me, kid."

"No, it's not."

"Well, of course, I didn't mean—I know your mother's going to get better and all."

"Gram's here too."

"Huh?" Dad actually glances, for the briefest instant, behind him, as if imagining Gram in the backseat of the car.

"Inside. She's inside me. You, too, for that matter." I am so tired. Worn out from everything. Too much emotion, too much sorrow. I don't think I can make my father understand how Gram is always going to be a part of me, but for some reason it's important for me to try. As if the understanding might save him.

"Yeah, I suppose so," he agrees slowly.

"She told me she was. Before she died, she told me. It was almost as if she knew . . ." My voice trails off.

"Knew what?"

---- THE TICKET ----

"I don't know. Not what was coming, I don't think that, but just that something might happen. To take her away, you know."

"You and your grandmother were close." He states it as a fact.

"She was always there."

He clenches the steering wheel so tightly his knuckles look white. We both know Gram was there for me when neither he nor Mama was. I sense the rebuke implied in my words, but I cannot take them back.

"Do you think Mama knows?" I surprise myself with this question, and I watch Dad as he tries to grasp what I'm asking.

"What? That your grandmother is dead?"

I nod.

He is quiet for a time. "I think she knows," he says slowly. "She doesn't want to, but she does. That's why I thought it was important for her to be at the funeral."

He drives in silence. I crack my knuckles noisily, knowing both my parents hate this habit. It will make my hands ugly, Mama always says. Who cares about your hands, I used to think, when you're ugly all over? But now I only think, who cares about your hands if Gram is dead and your mother's in an institution for the criminally insane?

"Is she going to be okay?"

"Sure she is," he says quickly, brightly, but his words ring hollow. "I don't know," he amends, "not for sure, but I think she will. She's come out of it before, you know."

When I speak, it is in a very small voice, tight with fear. "Is it hereditary?" I tremble while I wait for his answer, as though whatever he says will somehow prove itself to be true.

A flicker of recognition alters Dad's expression, and he appears disturbed but also strangely energized. The sky has lightened, and the sun pokes through a rosy cloud. The rain continues, however, and the cloud shifts position subtly, obscuring the sun once more. "No," he says, and then, "I don't know for sure." He chuckles, a sad sort of sound that comes out more like a sob than a laugh. "I don't seem to know very much today, do I? But the thing is, you're strong, Tray. Like your grandmother."

"I am *not* strong." I am furious at the suggestion. "And I'm *nothing* like her. I wish I were, but I'm not."

"She loved you very much."

"Don't tell me that."

"Why?"

"I don't want to hear it."

"*Why?*" he says again.

I am quiet for a long moment, trying not to cry while I think back to Gram's constancy and my meanness in return. "I know she loved me," I say finally. "I loved her too, but I hardly ever told her."

"You didn't have to. She knew you did."

"You don't know," I say, nearly shouting now. "You have no idea how mean I was to her. The things I said."

"None of us is perfect," he says quietly, and I wonder what memories Dad is wrestling with. Before I can think of a way to ask, he changes the subject. "Even if it—the illness, I mean—is sometimes hereditary," he says, "I don't think you have it. Try to put it out of your head."

"How old was Mama when she first showed signs of her—" (How do I phrase it: *her craziness, her streak of weird behavior, her ability to destroy*?) ". . . her problem?" I'm still hugging the side of my seat near the door, though not quite so tightly as before.

"I'm not sure. Did you ever ask your grandmother?"

"She didn't like to talk about it. I think she felt responsible or something."

"She spoiled your mother. She loved her too much, if that's possible. Loved her in the wrong way, I guess, but she was young herself and didn't know what she was doing. Perhaps Evelyn would have had all her problems anyway, no matter what your Gram did. I guess we'll never know."

We ride in silence for a while. The sky's turning blue now, but only in patches. Dazzling sunlit spots are popping in and out amid dark clouds. Is it the dark that magnifies the light or the other way around? Gram often told me to think of the glass as half full, not half empty, but I could never make up my mind

─────────── THE TICKET ───────────

whether I believed her. Are we better off to hope, even at the risk of having that hope crushed in a dark onslaught? The oncoming traffic is similarly undecided. One car has its lights on, the next does not.

Dad has switched the windshield wipers off and back on a dozen times. We're all undecided, I think, but how boring it would be if the future were known. "Why do you say I'm strong?" I ask abruptly.

"What are you reading these days?"

I stiffen defensively. "Why?"

"When I was a boy, I thought my father and I were as different as two people could be."

Puzzled, I release my hold on the door armrest and edge a fraction closer to him, curious to hear Dad talk about his past. This is something Gram does—*did*—but Dad hardly ever. I notice he's relaxed his death grip on the steering wheel too. He looks at me from time to time as he speaks, using his right hand to help express his thoughts. I often do this myself, another unladylike habit of mine.

"He was a farmer, you know, and he worked all the time and never seemed to have any money. Never dressed up in nice clothes or a suit. I wanted something so different. I didn't know how to make him understand.

"Back then, I figured everyone was the same down deep, that everyone wanted the same things out of life. He showed me how wrong I was. He had no desire whatsoever to wear a suit; he didn't care a flip about his image. Then, when I saw you all absorbed in a world of make-believe, I thought you were as different from me as I was from him. I was right . . . and I was wrong. We're all different, but we're also the same. Being the same isn't necessarily a good thing, but maybe it's not a bad thing either."

"What do you mean?"

"When I yelled at you for reading, I saw my dad in myself. I hurt you like he hurt me."

"How? How did he hurt you?" I move closer. There is now a distance between me and the door.

He grips the steering wheel once more, his knuckles white on it, pain dulling the moss green eyes. I think of the man at the tennis court, of the way I try *not* to think of him, and I wonder what things in my father's past might be like that.

"When your mother and I were first married," he says, "I was so young. Still a kid really. There was this Saturday when my daddy said we'd go fishing, and he chose the date himself. I thought maybe he was accepting me, letting me know it was okay I wasn't a farmer like him. Every day I was working—I hadn't gotten into insurance yet, I was selling door to door—I'd be telling myself that in just nine more days, and then just eight more days, and so on, I'd be on Kentucky Lake with Daddy, and he'd finally let me see that it was all right, that he was proud of me. I even imagined the words he'd say, to let me know how he felt. Days when I wasn't making any sales and my feet were aching, I kept on walking until my soles were paper thin, and that was what kept me going. The thought of being on that lake with him, rocking in the waves. And then, finally, it was just a matter of hours."

He hesitates, and I prod, wanting to hear and also afraid to know. "What happened, Dad?" Somehow I know from my own experience that when you look forward to something that intensely, you almost doom it to fail, one way or another.

"When I got there that morning, at five o'clock like we planned, Daddy was asleep. He seemed surprised to see me, and then he told me he'd forgotten all about it and made other plans. He told me to go on by myself."

"What did you do?"

"I did what he said. I went on by myself. I can still taste the bitterness of disappointment, not just at the lost day, but because of how foolish I'd been. Foolish to imagine him saying things he would never, ever say to me. That's why I'm so ashamed for doing the same thing to you."

"But you didn't, Dad. Not really. It wasn't that big of a deal."

"That's what I told myself that day. It's all right, I said. It doesn't matter. I can have just as much fun without him. But it did matter."

"What did you mean about the good part?" I ask, hoping now to redirect his thoughts. "How is it good that we're all the same?"

When he answers, his voice is unfamiliar, sort of hoarse and serious as if he's trying to be totally honest. I know this is a rare moment for him. For me, too. I think of the other moment, before the fire, when I almost told him and didn't. My head buzzes with confusion so that I almost miss what he's saying. Then his words break through the fog of my brain. "We're fighters, you and me and my dad. Whether we're making crops or sales or dress designs, we're made of the same stuff. It's a tough fiber, and it can withstand all the things that weigh us down and make us nearly give up." He punctuates his words with a wave of his hands. "And you, Tray, you're the best of us all. There was poetry in my dad—he saw beauty in his crops and in the soil and in the storms. I denied that part of myself, and maybe there is no more poetry in my soul. But there is in yours."

I am awed by such a speech from my father, who has never before shown any propensity for long or sentimental speeches, at least not in my hearing. Like *his* dad. And yet, for me, he has overcome his own nature. He stares straight ahead, and I wonder if he is embarrassed at having revealed so much. I feel pleased and humbled, but something obstinate inside prevents me from showing it. "So you're saying what? That I'm not crazy because you're not?"

"I don't exactly know what I'm saying. I'm sorry, that's all, I guess—that I got onto you for reading. And I'm sorry for leaving you at Lori's so long. And I'm sorry—" He starts to choke up. The hand that has been punctuating his speech drops like a lifeless puppet.

I do not know how to respond. I think of the way I could not bring myself to apologize to Gram for the hateful things I'd said, so I squeeze the hand on the seat between us.

There has been a subtle but powerful shifting, like sand beneath the tide, in the way I see things, the way I see us. I am no longer the unworthy, homely daughter of compact, beautiful parents. I cannot be sure whether my position in the hierarchy stayed fixed while theirs moved, or if all three of us have changed. I suppose no one can remain static for long.

Dad turns to look at me, a crooked smile playing at the corners of his mouth. Then he reaches up to brush away the tears from my cheek. Until then, I had not realized I was crying.

"There's so much for us to talk about," he says. It is as if a dam has broken loose inside him. "I've taken an apartment for us, but it's only temporary. I found one that didn't require a lease, so I just snatched it up. I should have asked you first, let you see it or something."

"What's a lease?" I think I know, but sometimes I get the wrong definition or assumption lodged in my brain, and I want to be sure.

"It's a commitment to stay for a year or more, usually, and I just wanted some place for us to live in while we decide what we want."

He's holding the steering wheel loosely now, with one hand. "Hey . . . do you still have that catalog?" he asks.

"What catalog?"

"You know, the one you showed me that had that blue outfit with the cashmere sweater—"

I am astonished my father remembers these details. The day I showed him the outfit feels like a hundred years ago. I nod.

"Maybe you can pick out a few of those outfits for us to order."

"*Really?*"

I know exactly which ones I will order, and I can just imagine the looks on the girls' faces at school when I show up in them. Then I think of the procession of sad-faced people pouring out their pleas, their needs so much greater than mine, and I say, "We should go shopping somewhere around here instead. I could probably find something on sale that isn't so expensive, and that way I could try it on to make sure it fits."

The lopsided grin lifts the corners of Dad's mouth again, and for a moment he looks young, the way he did before everything happened.

THE TICKET

"Speaking of sales, I've got another surprise for you." Dad reaches into the backseat and pulls forth a large plastic bag. It's from the department store where I bought my yellow and blue plaid skirt and fuzzy yellow sweater. Of course, Dad couldn't possibly know what I'd like, or my size, but I'm touched that he tried. I won't let him see if I'm disappointed, I tell myself as I reach inside.

I pull out a pleated blue-lavender skirt and sweater, the very one I tried on that same day when I settled for the other outfit. I check the size. Perfect.

"Dad!" I breathe. "How could you—how did you know?" I can't believe it was still there!

"Julia," Dad says. Julia. Of course. I feel sorry for every unkind thing I've thought about her.

"I gave her some money," Dad says, "but she deserves all the credit. She seemed sure you'd like this. Do you?"

"Oh, yes!"

"She wanted to give it to you herself, but I asked her to hold off. I wanted to see that look on your face myself. I hope that wasn't too selfish of me."

I'm holding the sweater, stroking the soft fabric. It's even lovelier than I remembered. I'm so grateful I'm speechless.

"It was on sale too," Dad says. "Julia said it was a great price."

Amazing. I remember how tacky all the clothes on the sale rack had seemed to me that day. I guess some things are meant to be as Gram always said they were. *Oh, Gram, I wish you could see me in this outfit.*

"Thank you, Dad!" I manage at last.

"I'm proud of you, Tray, for that honorable mention in the fashion contest, and for a hundred other reasons. I know I don't tell you that like I should. And I'm sorry you didn't win the big prize you were hoping for."

"It's all right." Now is as good a time as any: I broach the subject that has had us all in a tizzy for such a long time. "Have you decided what you're going to do with the lottery money, Dad?"

"No, I want us to decide together." I nod, caught off-guard. When I knew the decision wasn't mine to make, it was easy enough for me to think I would be generous. It made me feel superior in a way, as though I were above the lure of money. And yet, how I had longed to win the design contest. I was only fooling myself. My heart pumps furiously as the implications of Dad's words sink in. "Do you mean that?"

"I do."

THE TICKET

◊1960◊

CHAPTER TWENTY-NINE

When we get to Pee Wee's apartment, I'm struck by how meager it is. It makes our house, or what used to be our house, look like a veritable fountain of wealth, and I think how relative everything is. Even though there are all these kids at school with nicer clothes than mine, one thing I've learned from the whole lottery deal is how many people there are whose need is so much greater.

The apartment is up a flight of outdoor stairs. The railings are rusty, and the concrete on one of the steps is crumbling so badly it looks dangerous. I step over it, and Dad does the same.

While we're waiting for Pee Wee to come to the door, I look around the parking lot at the mix of cars. Most of them are in pretty bad shape, though there are a couple of exceptions. I recognize Pee Wee's bike, which is also starting to rust, chained to the stair rail.

Dad raps again, and Pee Wee cracks the door open. His hair is standing out around his head, even more erratically than usual, or maybe I've gotten used to seeing him in a baseball cap. He wears a pair of gray sweatpants and a faded navy tee-shirt. The sweatpants are baggy on him and bunch at his ankles. He's shoeless but wearing a pair of thick white socks with his big toe poking through a hole in the left sock. He looks startled to see us, almost fearful.

"Hey, man!" Dad says with an effort at cheerfulness and

─────── THE TICKET ───────

camaraderie I can tell is forced. Pee Wee must think so, too, because he doesn't look any more relaxed than before.

"Hi, Pee Wee," I say. He glances at me for a second, then quickly away.

"I don't mean to be rude," he says, "but I ain't ever been accused of having much in the way of social skills. So I'll come right out with it: What are you doin' here?"

"Can we come in?" Dad asks.

"Sure, sorry." Pee Wee lets us in, and a bluish-gray cat with a cream-colored throat and paws brushes against my leg. I bend down to pet the cat, surprised at how soft its fur is.

"Boy or girl?" I ask.

"Girl." Pee Wee looks apologetic. "I can shut her in the bedroom if you're allergic or anything."

"No, not at all." I continue to stroke her fur, and she purrs loudly. I've wanted a cat or a dog as long as I can remember, but Mama claims to have allergies, and I guess she does. "What's her name?"

"Buster."

"That's a funny name for a girl," I say.

Buster's ears perk in recognition of her name, and she stretches luxuriantly and rubs her paws on a carpet-coated scratching post. A few cat toys lie strewn about; a rubber mouse, a much-chewed ball of yarn, a bedraggled fake bird.

"She ain't got any front claws, but she don't seem to know that," Pee Wee says. "I named her before I knew she was a she, if you see what I mean."

We're still standing, and it doesn't look like Pee Wee is going to ask us to sit. So I drop onto the worn couch, and Buster jumps into my lap. Dad drops down beside me. There're a small table and two chairs in the kitchen area, which is just an extension of the room we're in. Pee Wee pulls one of the straight-backed chairs to face us, and straddles it.

"Sorry, it's kind of chilly," Pee Wee says. "I sort of got behind on my utility bills while I was—you know."

Outside the temperature is dropping. It is definitely chilly in here. In a way, I prefer it to Lori's overheated house, but it's likely to get pretty cold tonight, I think.

"We're sorry about that," Dad says. "For everything you went through. The thing is—why don't you tell him, Tray?"

"We want to share the money with you. Fifty-fifty." I'm absolutely thrilled to be able to deliver the news to Pee Wee, who so obviously needs it.

"No way. I couldn't take it." He holds up a hand in protest, but I can tell he's tempted. So I'm sure he'll change his mind. "It wouldn't be right," he says.

"Really, we both want you to have it," Dad says. "Like you told us all along, you deserve it."

"No. I don't."

"Of course you do!" I say. "We never would have won if you hadn't bought that ticket."

"I'm not taking it." He shakes his head vehemently. "And that's that," Pee Wee says firmly, and I'm less sure now that he's going to change his mind.

With the hand that's not rubbing Buster's back, I finger a small tear in the sofa, noticing that the apartment smells a little like cat. Must be the litter box. Mama always uses that as a second reason we shouldn't have a cat, no matter how many times I promise her I'll change it every single day. She doesn't believe me, and then there is that allergy issue too.

I keep stroking Buster's soft fur, and think how great it would be to have a pet, even for a little while. Maybe just until Mama comes home.

Pee Wee unwraps himself from the chair he's straddling, goes to his refrigerator, and sets out a bowl of milk for Buster. The cat leaps from my lap with a little meow and heads to the bowl. Her pink tongue darts eagerly toward the milk, whipping in and out. Pee Wee bends down to caress her back once, croons softly to Buster, and then moves toward the door leading outside.

I realize he's showing us out. Dad produces a check from his pocket, and Pee Wee gapes for just a second before he recovers himself. "I'm just going to leave this right here on the coffee

THE TICKET

table," Dad says, "and it will mean a lot to us if you'll accept it. With our thanks."

"The ticket only cost a dollar. That's all you owe me, and all I'll take. So if you've got a buck on you—"

"That's not what I'm thanking you for," Dad says.

"What?"

"The man at the tennis court," Dad says. He's sitting on the couch, and his hands clench into fists beside me. His face reddens. "Tray told me. We could never thank you enough for what you did there."

"But I threatened you and your family. There was no excuse for what I done. Let's call it even." Pee Wee opens the door, and a cold gust blows in.

"That's in the past," Dad says. "I'm ashamed it took me so long to see your point of view. It's only half. That leaves us with plenty. Plenty we'd not have without you."

"That's exactly my point." Pee Wee closes the door and turns back to face us. His eye twitches. "Plenty of trouble you wouldn't have had without me. Without my interference. That old woman. She was kind to me." For a second, I think Pee Wee is about to cry, and that makes me want to cry too.

"Like I said, I'm leaving that check," Dad says.

"Look!" Pee Wee stands in front of the sofa, eyes fiery, legs spread. "There's something you don't know." His eye twitches again.

He has our attention now. He looks from one of us to the other, licks his lips, opens his mouth to speak, then closes it again. "This is hard for me to tell. But it's been eating at me, so maybe it's providence you came here today."

"What?" Dad asks.

"I'm responsible for what happened at your house," he says. I freeze, and beside me, I can feel Dad stiffen.

"What do you mean?" Dad's voice is chilly now.

"Not like I started the fire myself, I didn't mean that exactly. I had time to do a lot of thinking while I was in jail. And I been blamin' folks for where my life went wrong when I should've been lookin' inside myself."

"So what are you saying—exactly?" Dad echoes Pee Wee's own word.

"I might've . . . no, I need to be one hundred percent honest here. It was me that put the notion of fire into your wife's—" He turns to address me: "Your mama's head. I taunted her. I didn't have any business bein' at your place, but I was. We were watching your neighbor burning trash together, and I said some words about people that start fires. I got the word wrong, and she corrected me." His eye is twitching steadily now, and he seems to be alternating between blaming and defending himself. "I was just trying to scare her, to make her think I might do something like start a fire. But she was in some strange sort of mood. I could tell she was, and I didn't know what to make of it. Not at the time. But now . . . now I'm pretty sure what I said pushed her over the edge, and—"

Dad leaps to his feet and lunges toward Pee Wee, poking his finger in Pee Wee's face. "*I ought to kill you.*" Dad growls, a sound I've never heard come from Dad's throat before, a sound that frightens me. Frightens me for Pee Wee. For Dad. For us all, for what we've become. Buster looks up from her milk dish, which she keeps licking, even though it's bound to be empty. She hisses threateningly.

Pee Wee, however, seems almost pleased by Dad's outburst, as if relieved to finally get his just deserts. "So you see why I couldn't possibly take any of the money. Not now."

Dad is not a large man, but just now he looks gigantic beside Pee Wee. Pee Wee's Adam's apple bobs up and down as he swallows hard, but he does not back away. In the split second before Dad's fingers seize his throat, I can see Pee Wee as he looked that day at the tennis court—larger than life and bridling with indignant anger toward the fat man.

As Dad's hands tighten around Pee Wee's neck, I jump to my feet on legs that tremble. I put a restraining hand on Dad's arm. As much as I miss Gram, as much as I, too, want to blame someone, anyone really, I know Gram would not want this. "Dad, don't."

THE TICKET

Dad turns to look at me, his eyes wild, then not so wild, then just sad. He loosens his grip, and his hands drop. "It was my job to protect Evelyn," he says finally, "and I failed."

"We all failed, Dad." I take his hand in mine.

Dad's hand is shaking inside mine, and his need gives me strength somehow.

"I'm sorry," he mutters and turns to face me. "You still want him to have the money?" he asks.

A hundred thoughts are racing through my brain. Pee Wee isn't all good, but he isn't all bad either. Like me. And Dad. Even Gram. We're all human, only human. I nod, feeling proud of Dad's faith in me, in my opinion. And, for once, I feel certain I've finally got it right.

As we pull out of Pee Wee's neighborhood, I look out the windshield, splattered with tiny drops of water, holding on for what is left of their existence. The drops crawl up the windshield, as if reaching for the clouds. "Look." I point to the sky, which has turned luminous. The clouds are edged in silver, and one teardrop-shaped cloud is golden against a suddenly vivid blue sky, as though the sun is smiling through tears. "You know what Gram used to say?"

"What?"

"When it's raining, and the sun is shining at the same time, it means it's going to rain again this time tomorrow."

"Your grandmother had a lot of superstitions like that. Funny thing was how often she turned out to be right."

"I miss her, Dad."

"Me, too." He glances at me. "That's another thing you were right about. She's still with us." He casts his gaze over his shoulder. "As surely as if she's sitting in the backseat of this car."

THE END

QUESTIONS FOR REFLECTION
The Ticket

1. Tray decides to lie to the police in order to help Pee Wee because she believes him to be wrongfully accused of starting the fire. Do you believe the "end justifies the means" in some cases? Is it ever okay to lie? Does Tray's lie serve the purpose she intends?
2. Tray feels guilty about things she said to Gram for which she never apologized. Do you think Gram forgives Tray? Do you think Tray forgives herself? Do you think God forgives Tray?
3. Gram likes to pass on wise sayings (such as her calendar's daily quotes) to her daughter and granddaughter. They do not always seem to be listening. Do you think the bits of wisdom make an impression on them anyway? Why or why not?
4. Tray worries that she might have inherited her mother's illness. Do you think she did? How can we keep ourselves from worrying about things we can't control?
5. Tray wants to be accepted by the popular gang at school so badly she is sometimes short with her friend Lori. After the incident at the bowling alley, do you think Tray still wants to be friends with Leslie, Candy, and Poppy? Why or why not?

6. In what ways is Tray like her father? Like her grandmother? Like her mother? Can you think of other characteristics that make Tray uniquely herself? Can you see traits of your parents or grandparents in you? When you recognize traits that you do not like, what can you do to change?

7. Why are Tray's parents so reluctant to share the lottery winnings with Pee Wee? Should they have split the money with him sooner? After he confesses everything he did to Tray and Jesse, are they right to share with him anyway? Would you have given him more or less?

8. Who starts the fire, in your opinion? Do you believe Pee Wee plays a critical role in the fire incident? Do his actions at the tennis court make up for his threats? Can we compensate for our mistakes with future "good deeds"?

9. Why doesn't Tray tell her parents about the incident at the tennis court? Why doesn't Gram tell them? Weigh the reasons for and against telling from Gram's perspective.

10. What sorts of mistakes does Gram believe she made in her marriage and parenting? What does she regret in her relationship with Tray? We all have regrets. How do we move past them? Do you believe that good can come from our mistakes? Discuss instances in the novel or in your own experience.

ACKNOWLEDGEMENTS

THANK YOU so much to Eva Marie Everson, who is my idea of all an editor should be; her lovely daughter Jessica and the rest of the creative team at LPC; my agent Les Stobbe; my publicist Jeane Wynn; my friend Betsy Johnson, who encourages me daily; and my academic colleague Paul Chaney, whose idea sparked the inception of *The Ticket* and whose diligence in revising our textbook allowed me to finish it.

Thank you to my loving and supportive family: my beloved husband Norm, who finds something positive to say about everything I write and who provided the Frank Norris quote at the beginning of the novel; my parents, Cliff and Marie Coleman, and sister, Jana Little, who make me believe they are always proud of me; my son, Clay Jeter, and Sarah Hagan, whose creative energies and artistic talents helped me in countless ways; and especially my daughter Nikki Wilbanks, whose faith in *The Ticket* kept me going and who has been with me every step of the way.